ABOUT THIS BOOK

Jetta Mills has felt stifled most of her life. She's a rebellious creative who's had to bend to her father's will, as well as the rules of her hometown, Havenwood Falls. Needing a break from it all, she skips town for an adventure far from the smothering influences she's used to. Unfortunately, trouble always has a way of finding Jetta, and she quickly learns that the best place for a frost dragon shifter such as herself is back within the warded borders of home.

When Conrad Monroe is hired to find a thief and bring her back to face justice, the trail leads him to the Colorado mountains and the path of Jetta Mills. She's gorgeous, talented, and a whole lot of trouble. He doesn't know what he's getting into with Jetta and the town she calls home. Jetta has no idea that Conrad has quite a few secrets of his own.

Jetta's seeking real freedom while Conrad's planning to lock her away. But sparks fly between the two as the line between deceit and truth quickly becomes blurred. When the smoke clears, the truth may be the only real path to redemption.

FLAMES AMONG THE FROST

A HAVENWOOD FALLS NOVELLA

AMY HALE

HAVENWOOD FALLS BOOKS

More books releasing on a monthly basis

Also try the YA line, Havenwood Falls High

Stay up to date at www.HavenwoodFalls.com

BOOKS BY AMY HALE

Ulterior Motives

The Shadows Trilogy
Shadows of Jane
Shadows of Deception
Shadows of Deliverance

Catching Whitney

Letters From Jayson

Havenwood Falls High
Somewhere Within

Havenwood Falls
Flames Among the Frost

For Sarai, and our mutual love of salad shooters.

CHAPTER 1

JETTA

I'd be lying if I said I'd never imagined myself in jail. I'd always been a hot mess with a talent for getting in way over my head. I'd never considered myself a bad person, but I was certainly no angel either. I always ran with the wrong crowd, said the wrong things, dressed the wrong way, and generally pissed off my father by merely existing. Lawrence Mills had been making my life miserable for years, although if you'd asked him, I'm sure he'd have told you the same about me. Despite my love for the rest of my family, I had to escape him. Which, in a roundabout way, was why my ass was going numb as I sat on a cold concrete bench in a six-by-eight cell.

"Damn," I muttered as I adjusted my position. "Hey assholes," I yelled, "are cushions against your religion or something? I can't feel my legs anymore."

I didn't expect an answer. It'd been six hours since I'd been arrested, and outside of my being booked, no one had spoken a word to me. My roommate, Frankie Hopkins, told me she'd be here to bail me out, but I'd yet to see her.

I stood and stretched, hoping to bring some of the feeling back into my limbs. The bland, gray cell was chilly, but actually the perfect temperature for someone like me—a frost dragon shifter. We generally preferred the cold to the heat. I guess when your roots traced back to

Iceland, loving the frigid temperatures made sense. It still pissed me off, though. The jackwads didn't even offer me a damn blanket. I think they hoped I would freeze. If so, the joke was on them.

The large metal door at the end of the hall opened, and I listened as footsteps approached. A uniformed officer and Frankie appeared on the other side of the bars. Her tall slender frame, shoulder-length red curls, and blue eyes were a welcome sight after hours of staring at the same cinderblock walls.

"About time," I growled, as the officer unlocked the door. His name tag read Barnes.

"You're free to go, Ms. Mills." Officer Barnes's expression appeared as if those words were painful to push past his lips.

I looked at Frankie, and she smiled. I shoved past them both and stalked down the hall to collect my personal items. The lady behind the window slid a paper bag toward me, and I inspected the contents. I grabbed the pen attached to the clipboard and signed to verify everything was there. Frankie held my jacket open, and I pushed my arms through before stuffing the bag into my pocket.

"May I go now?" I asked with more than a little disgust in my voice.

She nodded. Without another word, I walked to the main doors, Frankie on my heels. I pushed one door open, turned to face the officers standing in the lobby, and flipped them off. "Thanks for nothing."

Frankie rolled her eyes as she shut the door behind us. "Is it really the best strategy to piss off the cops who just arrested you?"

"Are you kidding me?" I glared at her. "Was I supposed to thank them for falsely arresting me, handling me like a piece of meat, and then ignoring me for hours?"

"Of course not," replied Frankie, "but being a bitch isn't going to help anything."

"But . . . I'm so good at it. It'd be a shame to waste my talents."

Frankie put one perfectly manicured hand on her hip. "And it wasn't exactly a false arrest. You did break into that safe, right?"

I didn't know how to explain what had happened. Partially admitting to the altered version of events would make more sense to her than the truth ever would.

"The item I was after belongs to me. I didn't want any of his other shit." I grimaced as I searched for her car in the now dark parking lot. "Thanks for bailing me out."

"Oh . . ." Frankie's voice was hesitant. "I didn't actually bail you out."

My eyebrows rose. "So, how'd you spring me?"

"It was Brandt. I talked him into dropping the charges." She looked nervous.

I felt my temperature rise. I shook my head as I found the nearest wall and leaned against it. As my eyes closed, I saw large claws, scales, and reptilian irises flash in my mind.

"Damn it, no!" I shouted in frustration.

Frankie placed a hand on my arm. "I'm sorry, Jetta, but I couldn't come up with the cash. I didn't know what else to do! I promise it'll work out. Brandt said he'd forgive everything that has happened. That's better than a bail bond, court, and a record, right?"

Frankie didn't understand that, while I was really pissed at her for working out a deal with Brandt on my behalf, the "no" was not about her negotiations. I was commanding my inner dragon to stay back. Being a shifter could be amazing at times, but this was not the time or place to let the beast come out to play. Anytime I felt threatened or upset, she tried to push through and take over. I couldn't allow that. Not again. I wasn't back home in Havenwood Falls anymore, where stuff like that was somewhat normal. This was Atlanta, and supernatural creatures of any kind were still considered part of myth and legend. My kind wasn't welcome in the human world.

I opened my eyes and released a heavy sigh. "So, what did you promise him?"

I quickly walked to her car, not waiting to see if she was following.

Frankie's heels clicked as she ran to catch up. "Not much. Just that you'd give him a chance."

"Oh hell, Frankie," I shouted.

"C'mon, just one dinner. Let him attempt to wine and dine you one more time. Enjoy an expensive meal, then brush him off and move on." She spoke as if her plan was simple, but she didn't know Brandt like I did. She didn't know I'd already been down that road.

"No one walks away from Brandt Sawyer if he feels he's owed something. It's why I'm in this mess to begin with." I frowned. "And now you're in the middle of it, too." I pushed my hands through my hair, still caught off guard by the length since having extensions put in. "Damn it!" I banged my fist on top of her car.

She unlocked the car, and we both climbed inside. "Stop being so dramatic. You act like you're dealing with a mobster or something."

I looked at her and wondered how she could live in such a big city all her life and still be so sheltered. "He pretty much is. He'll use our friendship against me."

"Oh shush." She started the car. "He's an arrogant, rich club owner, and your boss, but I highly doubt he's fitting anyone with cement shoes in his spare time." She rolled her eyes as she pulled out of the parking lot. "I know I haven't known you for long, but your paranoia has gotten really bad lately."

I shook my head. "It's not paranoia. The man is insane. He—" I cut myself off before I let my secrets slip. Frankie didn't need to know all the dirty details about my evening with Brandt. Or the reason it all went to hell. "Let's go home. I'm tired."

She nodded and steered us toward our apartment. We drove the rest of the way in silence, but once inside, I made a beeline for my whiskey stash. I opened the bottle, poured a healthy amount in a tumbler, and downed it in one swallow.

"It's gonna be one of those nights, huh," Frankie stated in a flat voice. She wasn't a fan of my drinking, but I'd made it clear from the beginning that I had vices and those vices would move in with me. Another perk of being a dragon—or con depending how you looked at it—it took a lot of alcohol to get us shit-faced. Thankfully I had a well-stocked bar.

"Yep," I muttered. "It's absolutely gonna be one of those nights." I poured another glass and threw it back, letting the comforting burn slide down my throat. "Do we have mac and cheese? I'm starving. Getting arrested makes a girl hungry."

Frankie jerked her thumb in the direction of the kitchen. "Cabinet."

I nodded and strolled the few short steps it took to travel from our living area to the kitchen, the whiskey bottle my constant companion.

THE ALARM CLOCK screamed in my ears. I rolled over and glared at the blue glowing digits. Seven a.m. wasn't terribly early, but it felt that way when you'd consumed all the alcohol in the house. I slammed my fist down on top, knocking the clock to the floor.

"Shiiiiiiit," I moaned loudly as I rolled over. My mouth felt like I'd swallowed a distillery. All I wanted to do was go back to sleep, but I really needed to run errands before rehearsals that afternoon. *Rehearsals! Work!* I bolted upright in bed as my mind reeled with the events of the previous night. Brandt. Our fight. The safe. Jail.

I couldn't stay here, not now. I slid from the bed and pulled my suitcase out from underneath. Tossing it on the bed, I unzipped it and made a beeline for the dresser. Without care or organization, I dumped the contents of my drawers into the suitcase, followed by my clothes in the closet. I had to sit on the lid to zip it shut, but after no small amount of effort, I managed to force it closed.

"I need to get dressed," I muttered as I realized I'd just packed everything. Out of the corner of my eye, I saw the clothes I'd worn the previous evening. Frowning, I looked them over. They were wrinkled, but even worse was the blood on the right sleeve and back of my shirt. I wasn't sure if all that blood was mine. Some of it may have belonged to Brandt. Both of us were injured the night before. Anger seethed beneath the surface. I had to take care of this problem before it became impossible to correct.

I pulled my bloody blouse on over the T-shirt I'd slept in and slid my legs into my jeans. I crammed my feet into my boots, not caring that I was without socks. I took a few minutes to pack the rest of my personal items scattered around the apartment, and then I hauled it all out into the living area near the door.

My eyes scanned the small two-bedroom apartment I'd been calling home for over a month. The dingy yellow paint, the kitchenette, the tattered secondhand furniture. I'd miss it all.

"What the hell are you doing?" Frankie whined as she stepped out of her room. She was rubbing her eyes and yawning, her red curls a wild mess around her head.

"I'm going home." I grabbed my jacket from the back of the sofa and put it on.

"What?" The shock of my announcement woke her up fully.

"I tried this. It didn't work. It's time to go back to Havenwood Falls."

She stepped forward and put a hand on my arm. "Are you sure? You hated it there."

I nodded. "Now, I hate it here more."

Frankie frowned, and I realized what I'd said sounded harsh. I pulled her in for a hug. "It's not you, sweetie. I love you. It's this city. I'm better off in a small community. And I can't be in the same area as Brandt. It's not safe."

Puzzled, Frankie sighed. "Okay then. I think you're overreacting, but do what you gotta do."

I slipped her a wad of cash. "This should cover my part of the rent for the next six months. That'll give you time to find a suitable roommate, and you won't have to accept the first weirdo that answers your ad."

She grinned. "You mean like I did with you?"

"Exactly." I smiled. "Don't let another freak cross that threshold. You were lucky with me. The next one might not be so great. Be picky."

She pulled me in for another hug. "I'm gonna miss you, roomie. You're weird, but I like that."

"I'll miss you too," I said softly. "I need to load this stuff in the Jeep, and then I'm out of here. Do not engage with Brandt or any of his goons, okay? Once I'm gone, he'll likely leave you alone."

She nodded. "Will do."

It took three trips to haul all my belongings to the Jeep. Once my stuff was packed away, I said a final goodbye to Frankie and pointed my vehicle in the direction of Sawyer's Bar. I'd been away from home for roughly 41 days. I'd tried to assimilate, but the time had come to accept defeat. I had one final stop to make before I put Atlanta in my rearview mirror.

CHAPTER 2

CONRAD

Smoke filled my nostrils as I walked into the dimly lit club. I allowed my eyes to adjust and then exhaled a slow, steadying breath. I'd always been sensitive to smells, but places like this violently assailed my senses. Sawyer's Bar was a sickening mixture of alcohol, sweat, tobacco, drugs, and bodily fluids. Thankfully I had developed a strong constitution over the years.

"Mr. Monroe?" A petite blonde with large blue eyes and a heart-shaped face appeared before my eyes.

"Yes, that's me," I stated.

"Mr. Sawyer is waiting for you in the back room. If you'll follow me, I'll take you to him." She flashed a nervous smile.

I nodded and waited for her to lead the way. The building was sparsely occupied. We passed between a long bar and a row of high-top tables before we reached a large stage. Instruments were placed at key points to surround a single barstool and microphone. At this time of the day, most people were still working or picking up kids from school. But here, people were slowly filtering in to drink their sorrows away. The musicians wouldn't start their evening shift for a few hours yet, so the only sounds were a faint playlist humming from the overhead speakers.

I followed the young woman through a door to the left of the stage, and we entered a hallway that was slightly darker than the main part of the club.

I willed my senses to stay alert, and I instinctively felt for the gun snugly stashed in the holster under my jacket. Assuring myself my weapon sat within reach, I made my way to the end of the hall and a set of double doors. The young woman knocked twice.

"Come in," a raspy male voice answered.

She turned the knob and pushed the doors open, motioning for me to enter. "Mr. Monroe is here."

"Please, have a seat. I'm Brandt Sawyer." The man behind the desk looked to be roughly my age. Maybe a year or two older than my thirty years. His short blond hair was combed to one side, and he had a scratch that trailed from his left cheek to the corner of his mouth. It appeared to be healing, but the mark still had that angry red hue that indicated it had been a recent injury. His smile was friendly, but something in his dark brown eyes set me on edge. I wasn't generally a trusting person, and I tended to keep most people at arm's length. This guy absolutely belonged in the "keep at arm's length" category. He reeked of bad decisions and arrogance.

I occupied the chair directly across from Brandt's desk and crossed my arms.

"How can I help you?" I asked. I'd never seen the point in making small talk.

Brandt's smile grew, his perfectly straight teeth gleaming back at me like some damn toothpaste commercial. "Direct. I like it."

He reached for a pack of cigarettes, pulled one out for himself, and then offered me one. I shook my head, giving his teeth a second glance. He must over-whiten to compensate for the tobacco stains. He lit the cigarette, and I steeled myself for the aroma that would permeate my nose.

"I have a bit of a predicament, and I'm told you are the man that can help me." He put the cigarette to his lips as he studied my face.

"I've been known to help people. It's part of my job. It does depend on what kind of predicament you are in, though."

"Of course," he stated. "So, I'll jump right to it. A disgruntled employee has stolen something very valuable from my safe. I want you to bring it, and her, back to me."

I sighed. "I'm not that kind of help."

I stood to leave.

"Wait, you need to hear the whole story."

I stepped away from my chair.

"I'll pay you a lot of money. And I do mean a lot."

His offer stopped me in my tracks. I hated working for guys like him. His type always thought money could solve everything—could get them whatever they wanted. It frustrated me, that in this case, he was probably right. I needed the money. Badly.

I sat back down. "You have five minutes to make your case."

He wasted no time. "A woman named Jetta Mills worked for me here at the club. She's been my main act for the past month. Very talented musician. A few days ago, I caught her breaking into my safe, and she attacked me."

My eyes flew to the scratch on his face.

He pointed to a large fire safe nestled in the corner of his office.

"I have friends at the police station, so I had her arrested, hoping to just scare some sense into her. No official charges were filed." He stood and turned to face a tall cabinet behind him, opening one of the doors. "I haven't seen her since." He turned back to face me, a folder in his hands. "When I came to the office the following morning, I once again found my safe open, and this time, important items were missing."

I shrugged. "So why not call the police again?"

He handed the folder to me. "Because they won't be effective. Not in this case. She's not your typical thief. I need quick results. The items she stole are time sensitive. Law enforcement's hands are tied by procedure."

I opened the folder and glanced at the contents. He had very little information to go on: an address in the city that was likely no longer valid; a description of the stolen contents, which were a metal lockbox containing some cash, jewelry, a sealed envelope, and a cell phone; and a photograph of the young woman he called a thief. She was a beauty, although something about her style seemed a little exaggerated. Her hair was long and dark, her eyes an icy blue, and she had a diamond stud in her nose. A ring decorated her eyebrow, and she had various other piercings in her ears.

"Is this all you have?" I placed the folder on his desk.

"Yes, at the moment." He sighed. "Her roommate claims to have told me all she can, although I suspect she's hiding something."

"So, you've already checked for her at that address?" I inquired.

"We did. Frankie, her roommate, said she'd packed her stuff and left town shortly after waking up the morning after her arrest." Frustration laced his features as he spoke. "Frankie knows very little about Jetta's past, but she did mention a hometown in Colorado. Something that ended in falls. She couldn't remember the exact name, but Jetta told her she was going home. My boys have been looking all over, but have found nothing that helps. I knew the time had come to hire a professional."

I mulled this information over a bit before speaking. "So, you want me to find her and return your items."

Brandt nodded. "And bring her back to account for her crimes."

"Did she skip bail?" I asked this knowing there wasn't any bail to skip if he hadn't pressed charges.

"No, but that doesn't mean she shouldn't be held accountable." I could sense his anger at the young woman.

"I'm mainly a bail enforcement agent. If she hasn't skipped bail, I can't legally detain her. You'd need the authorities for that. As you said, there are procedures." I stood once more, eager to get out into the fresh air.

"The friend that recommended you said you have ways of working outside the law to achieve the desired results. It's why I called you instead of the police." He snuffed his cigarette out with agitated movements, the well-used ashtray already full.

I didn't reply. I had been working hard to put my illegal activities behind me and make money by legitimate means. Renewing those pursuits didn't interest me.

"Like I said, I can pay you well." He opened a desk drawer and pulled out several stacks of cash wrapped neatly in rubber bands. "Fifty thousand. Twenty-five of it now, and the other half when you deliver my stolen items and Miss Mills."

I closed my eyes. I did not want to work for this man, but fifty thousand was hard to turn down. It would take care of my debts and leave me a little seed money to work with, so I could start over elsewhere. I needed out of Atlanta. My brain screamed at me. *Take it. One last quick and dirty job. Just this last one. Pay off your debts, and then you are done forever.*

"That's a lot of money. Are the items stolen really worth it?"

He pressed his lips into a thin line. "The contents of that box are priceless. It's worth any amount to retrieve them as soon as possible." He paused as he gave me a hard stare. "As well as Ms. Mills. It's important she returns to make things right. But that's not your concern. Just bring them back to me."

I reached for the folder. "Fine. I'll start first thing in the morning."

I hated myself. I hated that I could be bought.

Brandt smiled. "Fantastic." He placed the stacks of cash in a paper bag and sat them in front of me. "I want you to check in with me all along the way. Keep me apprised of your progress." He handed me a card. "This has my cell number. I can be reached here at any time."

I nodded and tucked the card into the folder.

He handed me the paper sack. "I'm looking forward to hearing from you soon."

I nodded again and left the room. My mind was already at work, putting together what little info I had and determining the best place to start my search.

Once outside, I inhaled a huge breath of air and blew it out slowly. I wouldn't exactly describe it as fresh, but breathing out there was ten times easier than inside of Sawyer's Bar.

I strolled to my motorcycle as I secured the folder and cash under my zipped jacket. The engine fired to life, and I smiled at the familiar and comforting rumble. I enjoyed the brisk twenty-minute drive to my small apartment, all the way wondering why this young lady had stolen from Brandt Sawyer. He was a rich, spoiled brat who had connections. Dangerous connections. She obviously hadn't known who she was messing with.

Once inside my living room, I powered on my laptop and did a search for Colorado towns with "falls" in the name. I found several, but I had no idea which would be correct, so I made a list of them all. I intended to speak to her roommate Frankie first thing in the morning. I also did a search on Jetta's name. I found zero results, which puzzled me. Almost everyone had some kind of online presence these days. She was a young entertainer. Surely, she had, at the least, a Facebook page or website. But my searches all came up empty, save for a couple of elderly women who were most definitely not my target. I leaned back on the sofa and closed my eyes, working to shut out all the noise of the city. I focused on the image in my mind of the woman I was now hired to find. Her smiling face was the last thing I remembered before falling asleep.

I KNOCKED on the door of apartment 28B and stuffed my hands in my pockets. I could hear faint movements before a deadbolt clicked and the door cracked open. One blue eye stared back at me over a gold chain that stretched from the frame to the door.

"Yeah? What do you want?" The woman was obviously cautious. Smart.

"I'm looking for Jetta. Is she home?" I flashed her my friendliest smile, hoping it would put her at ease.

"She moved." She looked ready to slam the door in my face.

"Oh no. Well, that's unfortunate." I did my best to mimic disappointment. "I'm Conrad. I'm an old friend of Jetta's. I was hoping to surprise her, but . . ." I let my voice trail off and shrugged. "This was the address she gave me a couple of weeks ago."

"Well, she's not here anymore." The tone of her voice held suspicion.

"Are you Frankie?" I asked.

She nodded.

"Jetta told me you two shared the place." I knew I'd have to play this carefully.

Frankie nodded again. "We did. Past tense. She went back home."

"Back to Colorado?"

Frankie's brows furrowed. "Yeah."

I scratched my chin. "She grew up in that town . . . oh shoot. What was the name?" I pretended to think and pulled random names out of the air. With any luck Frankie would help fill in the blank. "Woodward

Falls?" She didn't move a muscle. "No, that's not right. I was sure it was something like that. Cedar Falls? Rocky Falls?"

Frankie sighed. "Havenwood. Havenwood Falls. Can I go now? My breakfast is getting cold."

I nodded, and before I could push the word *thanks* past my lips, she'd slammed the door and locked it.

I smiled as I pulled out my phone and did a search for Havenwood Falls. I was surprised to see that name as the first result. It wasn't on my list. *Why didn't I see it when I searched yesterday?* I clicked the link and found myself temporarily pulled in by the gorgeous scenery. The home page was full of photos of a quaint little town boxed in on all sides by mountains and dense forest. A glance at the community calendar showed a busy schedule, jam packed with events all year round.

I shoved my phone back into my pocket and made a mental list of what I'd need to pack. Colorado in April was a bit colder than Georgia. I'd need to prep accordingly.

CHAPTER 3

JETTA

J pulled into the parking lot of Whisper Falls Inn and shut off the engine. I was exhausted. I'd driven it straight through, with only minimal stops, in fear that Brandt would follow me. I'd longed to stop at hotels for a few nights and see all the corny sights along the way. Who knew when I'd be able to leave Havenwood Falls again? After my experience in Atlanta, maybe never. I'd realized just how risky it could be for a supernatural being living outside the magic bubble of our town. Havenwood Falls was founded specifically to keep various non-human species safe. We did have human residents. Most of them had no idea that they lived among a variety of creatures they would normally consider monsters, but that was by design as well. My hometown was never dull.

The downside was that there were memory wards in place. Wards I had to convince a witch friend of mine to help me bypass, so I could come back home, should I wish to. I also asked her to concoct a spell that made my moves untraceable. I didn't want to be tracked, should I have decided the relocation would be permanent. Without the powerful ring given to me by my magically talented friend Ani Rukska, I would have succumbed to the amnesia spell that protected Havenwood Falls. It's kind of genius actually. Visitors who leave our little town forgot all about us once they passed twenty-five miles outside of the city limits. Their time here became more like a vague recollection or dream to them. For residents, the situation was a bit different. We couldn't be gone for more than a moon cycle. We only had twenty-eight days, or we lost all memories of home.

I left to break away from the constricting influence of my father. And I wanted to try something on my own. To take a huge leap and see where I landed. Sadly, I landed in the office of Brandt Sawyer. A step I sorely regretted. I hated coming back home with my tail tucked between my legs, but I knew I had made the right move. I was safe here. Brandt couldn't find me or Havenwood Falls. I could finally relax.

I glanced over at the metal lockbox sitting on the passenger floorboard. The contents of that box had to be well hidden. No one could ever find what I had pilfered from Brandt's safe. I closed my eyes and leaned my head against the steering wheel.

A familiar voice sounded next to me with "Long day?" and caused me to jump, a yelp escaping my lips as I turned to see Madame Luiza Petran sitting in the passenger seat.

"Damn it, Madame Luiza, you scared the hell out of me," I chastised.

"Good afternoon, dear. It's nice to see you, too." Her eyes twinkled as she spoke. "Are you gonna sit out here in the cold all day? We have some fresh coffee in the lobby, if you'd care for a cup."

"That would be wonderful. Thank you."

She smiled and then disappeared.

"Fuckin' ghosts," I muttered. Madame Luiza was a vampire who had run the large three-story Victorian manor for a while after her brother- and sister-in-law died. She'd passed away, too, and her ghost now haunted the place. I'd always liked her, but sometimes I thought she enjoyed surprising people a little too much. She was damn good at it.

I draped a blanket over the lockbox and slid out of my Jeep.

Once I reached the entrance, I steeled myself for the many questions I expected would be hurled at me, and then walked inside. I was welcomed by the familiar sight of polished oak flooring, beautiful stained-glass windows, and intricately designed rugs. The large manor had a comforting mix of Victorian era design and modern conveniences. Electric fixtures were now hanging in areas where old wall sconces had once existed. The heavy wood doors to the dining area hung from shiny new hinges, yet somehow still managed to creak as they moved, giving the house an ambiance that was often prevalent in older homes. Unexpected emotions rose from my chest and caught in my throat. I never would have believed I could miss Havenwood Falls so much. And this lovely inn was merely a small part of the town I called home. If only my father were a different man, I might have been perfectly content in this canyon.

"Jetta!"

I looked up to see Sindi Scott smirking at me.

"Where'd you take off to? Everyone's been looking for you." She raised one perfectly sculpted eyebrow. I hated how perfect her eyebrows were. My eyebrows looked like drug-crazed caterpillars compared to hers.

I shrugged. "I needed a vacation."

Sindi crossed her arms. "Liar."

I bit back a smile. Sindi was one of my favorite people since she'd moved to Havenwood Falls the year before. She was a sultry, redheaded goth vampire. She didn't bullshit, and I loved that about her.

"I checked out your old stomping grounds. Atlanta's a crazy place. But you're free to believe whatever you want. It won't change my answer to anyone who asks." I held up my credit card. "Do you have any rooms available?"

"We do. But why aren't you staying at home? Your father would be happy to see you." She took my card and began the registration process.

"My father is never happy to see me. Besides, I'd prefer not to see him just yet." My words were tight, and I hoped my tone didn't seem snippy. The mention of my father always made me pissy.

She shook her head. "You are so predictable, Mills."

I shrugged. "It's not a secret that Dad and I don't get along."

She handed me the room key and my credit card. "Let us know if you need anything."

I nodded and swiftly went back out to grab my things before anyone else had a chance to corner me.

I took a long, luxurious nap. By this point, I had no doubt that several people had spotted my Jeep and word had spread. Jetta Mills was back in town. The way I'd left, I'm sure there were those who expected to never see me again. Hell, I didn't know what I'd do once I passed the city limits. I just knew I had to leave. I was tired of fighting with my father over . . . well, everything. He hated my style, my attitude, my language, my music. Anything uniquely a part of me, he disliked with an intensity I could only describe as utter disgust. Of course, knowing this, I did all I could to exaggerate those characteristics. I'd acquired more tattoos, more piercings, and acted out more than ever. We engaged in a constant battle of wills, that old man and I. I was determined to win.

I showered and put on a fresh change of clothes before I looked myself over in the mirror. My black jeans were skin tight and ripped in several places. The gray shirt I wore had a wide neck and hung loose enough to expose all of my collar bone and part of my shoulders. My black boots shone, with the silver buckles on the sides catching the light when I moved. I loved those boots. The four-inch spiked heels alone could be considered deadly weapons.

I put my favorite silver hoop earrings in and smiled. Since removing the extensions and washing out the temporary dark color, I now had my natural silver hair back—an unusual color I'd had since I was a teen. I felt like myself again. The extensions were a fun experiment, but I missed my pixie cut, and the time had come for another trim. I was also happy to no longer need makeup to cover the tattoo on my neck. I'd worn long sleeves everywhere while in Atlanta, so my partial tattoo sleeves were hidden, but the dragon on my neck was unique, and I hadn't been comfortable letting anyone outside of Havenwood Falls see it. I wasn't sure why. Maybe some sort of instinctual protective mechanism took over—I didn't know, other than my gut told me to hide it, so I did. Frankie was the only person who had seen the beast that hugged my neck.

If I was being honest, I think a part of me knew that leaving home was risky enough that I should take some precautions. I'd almost changed my name as well, but decided that was taking it too far, considering our little box canyon was all but impossible to find if you weren't drawn to it by the town's magic.

I placed my usual rings on my fingers, except for the one Ani had given me. I no longer needed the protections it granted. I had to destroy the abomination before anyone learned of its existence and we both got into trouble. For the time being, the lockbox would keep my secrets.

I grabbed the box from the nightstand and sat it in my lap before I punched in the four-digit code I'd stolen from Brandt's desk. The soft click of the lock indicated the door was open. I raised the lid and froze. I allowed myself a moment to push down the bile that rose in my throat, then I tossed the ring inside and slammed the lid shut.

At that moment, a knock sounded at the door, and I pushed the box under the bed with haste. I moved to the door and unlocked the bolt, then opened it. My father stood on the other side, his tall, bony frame and piercing green eyes filling my vision. I looked at his bushy white hair and matching eyebrows and silently wondered if it'd take a hedge trimmer to get those suckers under control. His appearance was frailer than I'd ever seen him.

"Oh, it's you," I said.

"Yes, it's me." He pushed past me without invitation. I watched as his shrewd and critical gaze roamed the small room. His sour face made it obvious he didn't approve of the lodgings I'd chosen, even though the décor was beautifully done. Dark wood trim and floors mixed with lovely antique furniture and eggshell colored paint, and pastel lampshades, drapes, and linens accented the room, lightening up the heavy feel created from the darker furnishings. If my father hated this, he'd have died on the spot over my apartment in Atlanta. But his disgust was no surprise. He was a snob of the highest caliber. Nothing was ever good enough for Lawrence Mills.

I shut the door and leaned against it. I knew what was coming, and I braced myself.

"Where have you been, young lady?" His voice was stern, barely restrained anger at the surface.

"Not here," I replied as I crossed my arms.

"Don't be an idiot. If you'd been here, I wouldn't be asking the question."

I raised my eyebrows at him. "I think the idiot is the one asking the stupid question."

He growled, and the low rumble was a warning sign that he was about to lose his temper. While I'd love to see the always composed and proper Lawrence Mills shift due to anger, it wasn't fair to the other guests or the employees at the inn. Dad could make a mess when his temper flared.

"Chill, before you hurt yourself. I'll tell you." I motioned to the bed. "Have a seat."

He continued to frown, but he did as I directed.

"I took a road trip. I needed a change of scenery. I landed in Atlanta and got a job for a bit, then decided I was done with the big city life, and I came home. The end." I put my thumbs in the pockets of my jeans and rocked on my heels. "So, now that we're caught up, you can leave, and I can continue with my plans for the evening."

"Did you ever stop to think I might have been worried, Jetta?" His voice was low, but still held that hard edge I'd become accustomed to when he spoke to or about me.

"Not really. You have plenty here to keep you occupied. Especially now that Tristan and his family are back." I shifted my stance, eager to get out of the room.

"It's nice to have your brother back, although things with him certainly haven't gone as planned." He looked at me with those eyes that once held all the love in the world for his little princess. That love had been gone a long time.

"Well . . ." I drawled. "Maybe if you stopped trying to run everyone's life, you'd be less disappointed when they didn't march to your drum." I smiled sweetly, knowing my words and expression would irritate the hell out of him.

"Bah." He scowled and stood, relying on his cane more than usual. "I can't talk to you when you're like this." He hobbled toward the door, and I stepped out of his way.

"I'm always like this." I opened the door for him.

His hard gaze met mine. "I know." Then he walked out without a single glance back.

Well, that went well.

I grabbed my keys and locked up my room. My stomach rumbled, reminding me that I needed to eat. While I was out and about, I had a bartender to see.

CHAPTER 4

CONRAD

J pulled my truck into a little gas station just outside of Grand Junction and plucked a map of Colorado from the center console. I suspected the GPS was taking me in circles, and the sunlight was fading fast. I'd traced the route the GPS had been using and groaned. Yep, circles. I knew Havenwood Falls had to be somewhere close, but the GPS coordinates were screwed up, and the map didn't show it even existed. The GPS said my destination was nearby, yet no matter what direction I drove, I ended up back near Grand Junction. It felt like I was in the Twilight Zone.

The high-pitched squeal of brakes caught my attention, and I looked up to see a shuttle bus at the other end of the parking lot. The advertising on the side said, "Vacation in Havenwood Falls!"

"Hot damn." I tossed the map into the passenger seat and hopped out of the truck. I jogged over to the shuttle just in time to catch the driver as he disembarked.

"Hi," I said. "Are you going to Havenwood Falls?"

The driver smiled, the laugh lines around his eyes deepening. "I sure am. It's about time you got here. We'll be heading out in about twenty minutes. You need a ride?"

I shook my head. "What?" He must have had me mistaken for

someone else. "No, I have my vehicle. I'm just having a hard time finding the town."

He glanced behind me at my old truck. "That thing got four-wheel drive?"

"No," I stated.

His expression changed from friendly to concern. "Well, it might make it out there. Sometimes it's a little rough." He scratched his head a moment, then adjusted his cap. "You're welcome to follow me, if you like."

"Thank you. I appreciate that very much."

He nodded and looked at his watch. "We leave on the hour, so be ready to go."

"No problem."

I walked back to my truck and put the map away. The folder on Jetta Mills sat on the passenger seat, the corner of her photo poking out of the edge. I pulled the photo out and studied her face. Her beauty struck me again. Not a Miss America kind of beauty, but more like the sweet girl next door who had indulged in her bad girl tendencies. She didn't look innocent by any stretch of the word, but there was a softness in her face that spoke of the hopeful girl she once had been. Her ice-blue eyes were the kind a man could lose himself in, if he weren't careful.

I shook the thought from my head. It wouldn't do for me to lust after the target. I had to keep a clear head, especially if getting her back to Atlanta meant using illegal means.

"Shit!" I slammed my palm into the steering wheel. I hated that I was in this situation. No doubt, this would have to be the last time I took a sketchy job, no matter how much I was offered.

I wanted to take one more look at the Havenwood Falls website while I waited, so I searched it on my phone, but could no longer find it. No matter what I put in the search bar, there were zero results. I was starting to wonder if someone was playing some kind of elaborate prank with the place.

The bus pulled out of the parking lot, and I hurried to catch up. I stayed close behind it as we made the somewhat treacherous drive up, down, and around the mountains. When I saw the "Welcome to

Havenwood Falls" sign a couple of hours later, I breathed a sigh of relief. It did exist. I wasn't losing my mind. Step one down, many more to go.

The shuttle stopped at the town square. The quaint little area included walkways, a large fountain in the center, and a gazebo on one corner. I rolled down my window and signaled to an elderly gentleman getting off the bus.

"Excuse me. Can you recommend a hotel?"

His eyes squinted at me as he stepped closer. "Unless you're staying at the ski lodge, the only other place is Whisper Falls Inn." He pointed straight ahead. "It's on that corner."

"Thanks."

He nodded and continued on his way. I drove the short distance to the inn and put the truck in park. My wrist began to burn. I removed the brown leather cuff I'd always worn over a tattoo on my right wrist. I'd collected a lot of tattoos over the years, but I must have been really drunk when I agreed to that one. I didn't remember doing it. I couldn't complain about the quality. The tattoo was a Celtic triskele, roughly two inches in circumference. The three arms, made entirely of flames, swirled forward to meet the next. The artist did a great job with clean lines and subtle shading. For a colorless tattoo, the details were immaculate and well done. A triskele symbolized a balance between your inner consciousness and your outer self, but I had no idea why I chose one made of flames. Normally I would have loved a tattoo like that, but something about this one bothered me. I'd started wearing a cuff over it several years ago, and that had become habit. Every once in a great while, it would burn, similar to the sensation of a tattoo needle as it marked my skin—just as it did in that moment. I rubbed the spot with the thumb of my left hand and scanned the area outside my truck. The wind was picking up, and what few people were out and about scurried to enter the businesses that were still open. I put the cuff back on my wrist and ignored the stinging. It'd been a long day, and all I wanted was a warm bed and some uninterrupted sleep.

I WOKE up the next morning surprised to realize I'd overslept. I was generally an early riser, but the drive straight through from Georgia to Colorado must have wiped me out. I glanced at the bedside clock that said eight fifteen a.m. I sat on the edge of the bed and stretched. A shower sounded like heaven, so that was my first objective of the day. I allowed myself to soak under the hot water for just a few minutes before washing up and toweling off. I slipped on a long sleeve T-shirt with the AC/DC logo on the front, then pulled my jeans up over my hips. After slipping socks on my feet, I donned my boots. They were brown leather with a thick heel and steel toe. Perfect in my line of work, especially if head-busting was necessary. Bail jumpers didn't often go peacefully. I glanced in the mirror and gave my hair a quick swipe with my fingers, gathering it into a ponytail at the nape of my neck. My black hair was thick, and while I liked it long, I'd been keeping it no longer than my shoulders for the last couple of years; I preferred ease over length.

I took a moment to run my fingers through my neatly trimmed beard as well. I was thankful it mostly hid a one-inch scar that ran down the right side of my lower lip. Another injury I didn't quite remember.

"You gotta quit drinking," I said as I glanced at myself one last time before walking to the door. I swiped my keys and wallet off the side table, stuffing them into my pocket, then grabbed my cuff and put it on my wrist, wondering once again why the crazy tattoo burned at weird times.

I had just made it down the stairs when I felt a firm pinch on my ass.

"Whoa." I turned around. My mouth opened, but nothing came out. Behind me was the sweetest looking woman. Her gray hair shone, and she wore a purple gown. She smiled at me as if all she'd done was wish me a good morning. I snapped my jaw shut, turned back around and hurried out the door. I was sure I hadn't imagined that pinch, but I couldn't fathom the older woman doing it either. Just before the door shut behind me, I heard the girl behind the registration desk say "Madame Luiza!" as if to scold her.

I shook my head and grinned as I grabbed my jacket from my truck and slipped it on. *Time to do some digging into the life of Jetta Mills.*

I'D SPENT all day wandering Havenwood Falls. On the surface, it certainly appeared to be a nice little town, although all towns had their undesirable components. The people seemed friendly enough. I knew I couldn't just blurt out that I was looking for Jetta. If word made it back to her, and in a small town like this, it always did, she might bolt, and I'd have to start my search all over again. My best strategy was to blend in as a tourist, get to know the people for a few days, and keep my eyes and ears open at all times. Someone would eventually say something, or I'd see her. Finding her was inevitable. She was a beautiful woman, so it wouldn't be hard to fake interest in her and hopefully gain a little of her trust.

I'd heard someone mention that the Mills family had a large house in the fancy part of town up the hill, so that was information I stored away for later. I'd also heard that Simple Treasures Pawn Shop was owned by her family, so that was my next stop.

I opened the door and stepped inside. The store was brighter than I'd expected, with two-tone walls of gray and white, separated by a black chair rail. The wood floor had been polished until it shined. The overhead lighting appeared to be LED, and it gave off more of a nice jewelry store vibe than that of a place where people hocked stuff out of desperation. One side of the room had a long glass case with everything from jewelry to collectibles. The other side contained shelves of all sizes. Delicate dishes shared a shelf with vases, small statues, and those geode rock things that seemed to be so popular. Another section of the room, near the back, had instruments neatly lined up, as if waiting for a concert to start.

"Hi, are you looking for something in particular?" a young female voice said from behind me. I turned to see a teen girl with white-streaked dark hair and blue eyes. Her smile was friendly, so I returned her greeting.

"I'm new in town and just looking around." My words were clipped, and I had to remind myself, for the hundredth time, to be more outgoing. Being my usual reclusive and suspicious self wasn't going to win me any favors. Old habits die hard. I stuck my hands in my jacket pockets and glanced around the room some more, looking for anything that might interest me. I needed a reason to hang around for a bit without seeming creepy.

"Are you here on vacation?" she asked.

"Yeah. Although if I like it enough, I might consider staying." I spoke slowly this time, making sure I didn't rush my sentences. I walked toward the jewelry case and glanced inside. "Do you like living here?"

She moved behind the case and nodded. "Oh yeah. It's an awesome place to call home." She studied me for a moment, then stuck out her hand. "I'm Zoey."

I shook her hand. "It's nice to meet you, Zoey. I'm Conrad."

I prayed I didn't sound gruff. I was told my demeanor could scare small children. If I sounded like a jerk, she didn't seem to notice. She continued to smile at me.

I kept my eyes focused on the contents in the case. Her cheerful attitude was making me uncomfortable. I never had been good with kids, even when I was a kid.

My eyes roamed a row of thick rings, and I bent down for a closer look.

"Aren't those cool?" said Zoey. "My grandpa has a lot of items flown in from all over the world. Some of those rings are really old."

My eyes snapped to one ring in particular, and a lump caught in my throat. The silver ring was flat on top with an insignia embossed into the metal. An image that matched my weird wrist tattoo exactly. *What the hell?*

I pointed to the ring. "Can I see that one?"

"Oh, I really love that one. I tried to buy it once, but my dad said it wasn't meant for me." She huffed out a frustrated breath. "He's so picky about what I wear." She turned and pulled a set of keys from a drawer. After unlocking the case and sliding the door back, she pulled the ring out and laid it on a blue velvet pad, placing it in front of me.

I leaned down and inspected the ring, but didn't dare touch it. I wasn't a superstitious person, but I believed, for at least a few moments, that if I touched it, something bad would happen.

"Yeah, that's cool," I mumbled.

"Wanna try it on?" Zoey's enthusiasm for making a sale had me biting back a true smile.

"No, thanks. I just wanted to see it up close." I glanced at her. "Do you know the origins of the ring? Or what the symbols mean?" I was oddly desperate for an answer that would clear up my confusion.

"Not really. My dad and Grandpa are the ones that deal with most of that."

"Zoey? Honey, who are you talking to?" A man who appeared to be in his mid-forties stepped from a room in the back of the store. "Oh, so sorry. Didn't realize we had a customer. Has Zoey taken care of you?" He smiled at the teen.

"Yes, thank you. She's been very helpful." I couldn't keep from stealing another glance at the ring still sitting on the counter.

"Ah, I see you're interested in a very unique ring." He smiled as he walked toward us.

"I've never seen one like it. Zoey thought you might know its history." I put my hands in my jacket once more, resisting the temptation to pick up the ring.

"Oddly enough, I don't. It's a Celtic triskele, which in and of itself isn't unusual, but the flamed arms aren't anything I've seen before." He picked the object up. "Admittedly, I haven't had a lot of time to investigate it, so I've likely just not stumbled across the right information yet." He held the ring out to me. "Is it your size?"

I backed up, unable to avoid the ludicrous reaction. "I don't think so." I glanced at my watch. "I need to run, but it was nice to meet you both."

The man smiled. "Please come in anytime. You've met Zoey, but I didn't introduce myself. I'm her father, Tristan Mills."

I nodded. "I'm Conrad Monroe. Thanks again for the hospitality." I flashed them one last nervous smile and slipped out of the store, my heart racing in my chest.

"What the hell was that?" I whispered.

CHAPTER 5

JETTA

"Simon, c'mon man. You owe me," I grumbled, adding a little female whine in for good measure.

He raised an eyebrow at me. I'd considered flirting, but I'd learned a long time ago that strategy didn't work with Simon. He only had eyes for his boss Odette Alverson, the owner of Fallview Tavern & Grille. The fact that he was a dragon shifter and she was a siren didn't seem to deter him in the least.

"Seriously, I need a job. I don't want to live off my father or his money. I need to get back to making my own way before I run out of savings." My elbow was on the black marble bar, and I placed my chin in my hand and tilted my head. "Please?" I begged.

He nodded. "Fine. I'll tell Odette you're the new entertainment. I think she was getting tired of the old act anyway. You can work the off nights for now, and we can phase the other group out in time."

"Thank you!" I leaned across the bar and hugged him.

Simon blushed. "We're even now, though. No more bringing up how you helped me settle here and all that noise."

I nodded. "You got it." I flashed him a wide smile. "You love me. You know you want me around."

He shook his head. "I don't know. You didn't even tell me you were leaving town. I had to find out from your very angry father, when he came looking for you. He was sure I was holding out on him. And then you didn't bother to let me know once you were in town again?" He shook his head. "Not a lot to love about that."

"I didn't say anything so you could plead innocent when Dad came around, as I knew he eventually would. And I did come to see you last night, but you weren't here."

Simon sighed. "You're one of my closest friends. But I need you here like I need a third eye." He crossed his arms and gave me a stern look. "No troublemaking."

I nodded in agreement.

He narrowed his eyes at me. "You agreed to that way too easy."

I shrugged. "Maybe Atlanta changed me. Maybe I'm not the rabble rouser you once knew."

He snorted. "No one will ever buy that. Try to sell me something else."

"Fine. I need the work, so if I have to be on my best behavior, I'm willing to at least attempt it." I fidgeted with the silver skull ring on my index finger.

He nodded. "That I believe." He poured a beer and slid it across to me. "Be here at eight sharp. It'll be nice to hear some decent music again."

I took a sip. "Only decent? I must be losing my touch."

Simon sighed. "You do plan to leave soon, right? I have work to do." He sounded annoyed, but he winked at me.

"As soon as I finish this beer." I tilted it back and chugged it quickly.

He shook his head at me. "Ya know, normal girls don't guzzle booze."

I slapped some money on the counter. "I'm not normal."

He let out a full chuckle then. "Damn straight."

I slid off the barstool and gave him a wave as I strolled to the door. "See you tonight."

I stepped out into the bright sunlight and allowed my eyes a moment to adjust. I had a few hours before my first set at the bar. It'd been forever since I willingly let my dragon out. I needed to visit the falls.

I CAREFULLY TREADED the natural stone steps that led to one side of Smalls Falls. My favorite spot was some distance from the falls near Fallview Tavern & Grille, but this particular waterfall had special meaning to me and my family. Just behind the rush of cool water that spilled over the cliff, there was a small, very dark cave. At least, to the non-dragon eye, that's how it appeared. In truth, a large cavern that led deep back into the mountainside hid behind the falls. This was the Mills family cave, and my father had had it warded over a century ago so that our private retreat would stay a secret. We felt comfortable shifting into our dragon form in this cave. The large space had been especially great for learning, and I had recently taken my sixteen-year-old niece, Zoey, to the cave to practice shifting. It was scary for her, but she took to it quickly, and I'd been so proud of her.

I pushed my hand through the inky darkness and let out a contented breath as I walked the rest of the way inside. Home. This cave had always felt like home, no matter what else was going on in my life. I pulled a lighter from my pocket and lit the candles that lined the walls of the first room.

For a moment I stood there, basking in the sounds of rushing water while I inhaled the earthy scent that surrounded me. Then I heard soft sobs coming from the larger room.

I cautiously made my way to the next entrance and noticed a single candle sitting on the dirt floor, next to my niece.

"Zoey?" I whispered.

Her head snapped up, and she wiped a tear from her eye. "Aunt Jetta?"

I stepped forward. "It's me, sweetie. What's wrong?"

She stood and ran into my arms, wrapping hers around my torso in a big hug. "I'm so glad you're here! I missed you!"

"I missed you, too." I tilted her face to look at mine and noticed the dirt-streaked smudges on her cheeks. Tears had cleared small trails from her eyelashes to her chin. "Why are you crying?"

Zoey stepped back and inhaled a deep breath. "I had a fight with Jordan."

I frowned. "What happened?"

29

"It was stupid, and it was my fault. I got jealous over something petty." She sniffled. "And now I may have ruined our relationship."

I pulled her back to me for a hug, and I stroked her hair. "I'm sure you didn't. You just need to talk it out. Remember what I told you? Relationships only work when there is communication."

She nodded. Then, as an afterthought, she said, "Where have you been? I came here hoping I'd find you, even though I knew you'd left town."

Guilt landed like a rock in my stomach. I should have been there for her. At the least, I should have kept in touch with my brother. Tristan was one of the few people not intimidated by my father. "I'm sorry, sweetie. I should have checked in. I just needed to some downtime for a bit. Clear my head."

She sniffed again. "I understand."

"I'm sorry I haven't been here for you." I released her and stepped back. "It'll all be okay, though. I bet Jordan is feeling just as bad as you are about the argument."

"You think? I mean, he shouldn't. It was my fault." Her lovely blue eyes were so full of hope, it almost broke my heart. She was such a sweet young woman. So much the opposite of me.

"Maybe, but I doubt he enjoyed fighting, regardless of the cause. Call him when you get home. Apologize if needed. Talk it out."

"Thanks, Aunt Jetta. I feel a little better."

"Good. Now, you know what would make us both feel better?" I gave her a sly grin.

She looked up at me, and a slow smile replaced her frown. "Flying?"

I held up my hand for a high five, and she met mine with enthusiasm.

"First one to the top of the cliff is a bloodsucker!" I yelled, as I ran to the back of the cave while pulling my shirt over my head.

"Hey now, my best friend is a bloodsucker," Zoey said in mock offense.

"Sorry, not the vamp family I had in mind." I'd instantly envisioned the Roca brothers and their many escapades.

I kicked off my boots and peeled off my jeans, folding them neatly to place beside my shirt.

Zoey stood next to me, undressing as well. "Hey, we need to make ourselves Velcro clothes or something. I'm so tired of having to undress. Wouldn't it be cool to just shift, and our clothes fall away?" She smirked.

"So, like the Hulk without the tearing?" I asked.

"Yeah! Like that."

I chuckled. "Sure, we should work on that. For now, we'll have to be content with undressing so we aren't running around naked afterward."

I stepped back, assuring I had plenty of room and had left Zoey her needed space as well. Then I closed my eyes and summoned my dragon. I saw a quick mental picture of my shifted self—white scales with a bluish tint that matched my eyes; large jaws containing smooth and serrated teeth; claws, wings, and a tail at least half the length of my forty-foot-long body. My head crowned with a regal row of horns that started from the back side of my jaw and wrapped around behind my head, meeting the other side in a mirror image. Next, the stretching and popping began. The pain of my limbs elongating and bulking up was always there, but I'd become so used to it that I hardly took notice anymore. I opened my eyes as my vision clouded temporarily, then cleared to an almost telescopic vantage.

I looked down to see my beautiful niece as she began her own transformation. She made a few uncomfortable sounds, but the general act of shifting didn't appear to cause her a lot of trauma. It had always brought me relief to know young dragons didn't have the excruciating pain that older dragons experienced. I'd been told a gene evolved over time so that we wouldn't fear shifting. I'd always equated it to procreation. If the actual act were extremely painful, no one would do it, and the species would die off. I'd believed shifting was the same way. If the process was terrible, our younger generation may purposely choose to avoid shifting. Over time, the dragon gene could die off as we evolved once more. But that was just my theory. It wasn't like we had the world's greatest minds trying to figure it out.

When her shifting was complete, I lowered my head to hers and gave her a nuzzle with my snout. Some of my favorite times with Zoey had been in our dragon forms. She was a great kid, but she had a little wild spirit in her too, and that side I resonated with very well. She could be that side of herself when she let her dragon take over.

I pushed my enormous head through the falls, immediately triggering my camouflage so that I blended in with my surroundings. The frigid water felt fantastic on my neck, so I allowed it to run over me a moment before a hard nudge from behind alerted me to Zoey shoving at my tail with her head.

"Okay, I'm going." I laughed as our telepathic communication took over.

I stepped out, clearing the way for her, and she followed immediately. We both gave our wings a good stretch, then I glanced at her, noting the faint outline of her camouflage and the light puff of frost escaping her nostrils. Without her camouflage, she was a carbon copy of myself, only instead of twenty feet high, she was closer to fifteen. She also had the most mesmerizing iridescent scales. At times, I'd been a little jealous of her coloring.

I smiled, as much as a giant reptile can, and said, "Race you to the top!"

I hit the bank running, pushing my way through the dense forest. Unable to fully spread my wings, I tucked them in close and lumbered up the mountainside toward our favorite cliff. I could hear Zoey directly behind me. She'd gained some speed since our last outing and appeared to have no trouble keeping up.

Just as we'd reached the clearing that led to the edge, she zoomed past me in a blur.

"Holy hell," I muttered.

Once I reached her side at the precipice, I huffed out an annoyed breath. "So, where'd you learn that speed, kiddo?"

"You're not the only dragon who can teach me stuff, ya know," she teased.

"I'm getting old," I complained.

"Nah, it's just hard to compete with my awesomeness."

I chuckled. "So true." I leaned my head forward and looked down. "Shall we?"

"Let's," Zoey said with excitement. She obviously loved the freedom of flying as much as I did.

We both leapt off the edge, letting our wings work as gliders and slow our descent, then we tilted ourselves toward the sun, and with a powerful push from our wings, we were both rising among the clouds.

We spent a few minutes just enjoying the wind rushing past us. The cool, crisp air was invigorating. No matter my troubles, flying had always given me a respite. It allowed me a moment to breathe. That moment was about to be interrupted by Zoey's incessant matchmaking.

"Hey, Aunt Jetta," she sang in a high-pitched voice as she zoomed by me. "I met this cute guy at the shop today. He'd be perfect for you."

CHAPTER 6

CONRAD

I rolled my eyes as my phone buzzed for what felt like the billionth time. I pulled it from my pocket and slid the bar on the screen to answer it.

"Conrad," I stated.

"I've been trying to reach you." Brandt's annoyed tone assailed my ears.

"And?" I didn't appreciate being badgered, even if this was the guy paying me.

"And you haven't given me an update! It's been three days since you left Atlanta. What progress have you made?"

My eyes narrowed at accusations in his tone. "First, I don't care how much you are paying me. Talk to me with that attitude again and I'll break your face. With your own fist." I gave him a very brief moment to let that sink in. "Second, when I have news worth sharing, I'll let you know." I hung up on him.

Within seconds the phone buzzed again, and I turned it off. To be honest, the cell service here was shit anyway, and I fully planned to use that annoyance to my advantage. His impatience could have sabotaged my plans to bring her back peacefully.

I pushed my phone back into my pocket as I walked through the door of Fallview Tavern & Grille. The place was packed, and the only open seats were a few spots at the end of the bar, farthest from the stage. I settled in and flagged down the bartender.

"What can I get ya?" He eyed me curiously.

"I'd love a beer." I pulled cash out of my pocket.

"Sure." He took a few steps backward and placed an empty mug under the bar gun. A push of a button dispensed my favorite beverage. He slid it to me and took the bills I'd placed on the bar.

I took a swig and sighed. That was some damn good beer. I looked up to see the bartender staring at me.

"Can I help you?" I did my best to keep the irritation out of my voice. It wouldn't do to start a fight on my first real night out. The plan was to make friends, not alienate them.

He smirked. "I'm Simon Turner." When I didn't reply, he continued. "How long have you been in Havenwood Falls?"

"A couple of days," I countered. "My name's Conrad."

He nodded. "Well, welcome to our little canyon, Conrad." He busied himself with an empty glass. "Have we met before?"

I froze. "No, not that I can remember."

"Yeah, probably not. You just seem familiar."

The strum of a guitar caught my attention, and I shifted my eyes to the stage. A petite young woman with short silver hair sat on a stool, acoustic guitar in her hands. My distance from the stage made it a little difficult to see her clearly, but I could see the glint of piercings. When she turned her head, there was a large dark marking on her neck. I could only assume she had some kind of tattoo. I smiled. I liked her already. Then she began to sing, and my heart seemed to follow the rhythm along with her.

> You look, but you don't see me
> My soul vacant and stark
> Darkness the only friend
> I can trust with my heart.
>
> If I could show you clearly,
> The true me far beneath,
> Would you run? Could you embrace me

35

As reality bared its teeth?

Until then I'm transparent,
The illusion kept intact.
One day you'll see what no one can
And I'll finally be more than that . . .
Transparent.

Her voice was beautiful, with an edge to it that made me think she could easily slip between soft ballads and heavy metal. It suddenly occurred to me that she could be my target. But this woman's appearance was very different from the photo I had in my truck. I caught Simon's attention.

"Who's that?" I nodded my head in the direction of the stage.

"Ah, that's Jetta Mills." He shook his head. "If you're looking to take that one on, you'd better buy life insurance. She could eat you alive."

I chuckled and tried to hide the adrenaline rush of knowing my target was within reach. "Sounds like my kind of woman."

I took another drink of my beer.

"I can introduce you, if you'd like." Simon glanced her way. "She's a good friend. My only condition is that you don't blame me for anything that happens after that introduction."

"Sure, I can live with that." I was overly eager to meet this unusual young woman.

I sat at the bar for the next couple of hours, listening to Jetta perform and getting to know Simon, in between his various duties at the tavern. He was a likable guy, and if the situation were different, I could see us being friends.

As Jetta thanked the audience and slipped the guitar over her head, Simon leaned across the bar. "She'll come over for a few drinks before she heads back home. Her favorite drink is whiskey."

I nodded. "Gotcha. What brand?"

Simon's eyebrows rose in unison. "All of them."

"Damn," I whispered.

"Exactly." He put a shot of whiskey before me. "Enjoy."

Jetta made her way through the patrons seated in the bar, taking the time to say hello to each one, with the exception of one guy who appeared to have grabbed her inappropriately. I didn't see the full exchange, but I did witness the right hook she rewarded him with. He went down like a sack of potatoes.

Simon came around the bar and walked to where the guy slumped on the floor. "Damn it, Jetta. It's your first night. Did you have to punch a customer?"

She put her hands on her perfect little hips. "I sure as hell did. Next time he wants to get to second base, he should make sure he's on the right field."

She stomped toward the bar, and I turned my attention back to my drink. Taking her back to Atlanta would suck. Not because I didn't like her, but because I did. I couldn't say I'd met many women like her. Truth be told, I'm not sure I'd ever met any women like her.

She approached the bar, climbed up on a stool two seats from mine, then leaned over the bar and grabbed a glass. She picked up the bottle of whiskey Simon had just used to pour my drink, glanced at the glass in her hand, then promptly returned the glass to its previous spot. She put the bottle to her lips, and for a moment, some very erotic images came to mind.

I held up my shot toward her and said, "Cheers."

She nodded and took another swig from the bottle.

"That guy step out of line?" I nodded my head in the direction of the unconscious man Simon was dragging to the door.

She glanced over, then rolled her eyes. Eyes that were every bit the soft blue of the photo Brandt had given me. "He's used to it. He tries to feel up everyone when he's drunk. I'm just one of the few who refuses to put up with it."

I smiled. "Well done."

She turned to face me. "Really? Most men are intimidated by a strong woman."

"Nah, I like it. It's rare."

She looked me over, and then one side of her lips quirked upward. "Obviously."

Simon took his usual place behind the bar and poured a soda. "I see you two have already met."

37

I shook my head. "Not officially."

"Jetta, meet Conrad. Conrad, Jetta. There, now it's official." Simon took a sip of his drink and watched Jetta closely.

She nodded an acknowledgment and held up her bottle. "To new friends."

I held up my shot, which Simon had so thoughtfully refilled with a different bottle, since Jetta had commandeered the other one. "To new friends."

Simon held up his own. "To you two getting the hell out of my bar soon so I can close down."

CHAPTER 7

JETTA

*S*imon shooed Conrad and me out of the bar rather hastily. Something was up with him. I'd known him long enough to sense when he was hiding something. In the past, he used to love my company while he closed things up. He obviously liked Conrad. Why did he kick us out like he'd rather chew glass than look at us? I'd get to the bottom of it eventually. I always did.

As for Conrad, well, he was an enigma in tight jeans and a leather jacket. And had some seriously sexy brown eyes. I'd always been a sucker for the biker look, and he wore it very well. He could have easily fit in with S.I.N., our local motorcycle club. His dark hair was pulled back in a ponytail at the nape of his neck. His neatly trimmed beard blended seamlessly with his sideburns and had tiny flecks of auburn infused here and there. His mustache matched perfectly as well.

He caught me staring, and I smiled. I didn't care. He was hot, and I had perfect vision. Nothing wrong with enjoying the view. As long as he was only in town for a short while, I saw no harm in hanging out with the sexy tourist. I gave up on long-term relationships ages ago, so occasional flings were more my style. Of course, that would be after I made sure he wasn't some kind of nut job. I was fortunate that I didn't have to be quite as paranoid as most single women my age. I could simply shift and eat him if he turned out to be a psycho jackass. At that thought, another psycho jackass came to mind. The one I ran from back in Atlanta. I should have eaten him.

"Hey, are you okay?" Conrad asked.

"Yeah, I'm fine." I shook the image from my mind.

"You looked a little sick for a moment." His concern was obvious in his voice.

"Yeah, I'm good. Just dealing with some memories. Must have been triggered by the groping back there."

He frowned. "Did someone hurt you?"

I chuckled. "No, not really." *Not in a way you'd ever believe.* "But thanks for asking."

I wrapped my arms around my torso, and an involuntary shiver ran up my spine. I wasn't cold, even though my jacket wasn't lined. But the memories of what I had encountered were troubling. I felt Conrad's jacket wrap around my shoulders in a gentlemanly gesture.

"Thanks, but you'll get cold if you don't wear yours." I shrugged it back off and handed it to him.

"I'm actually comfortable at the moment." He draped the jacket over his arm as if it proved his point.

I couldn't tell if he was lying or not. As we walked to our vehicles, I watched for any signs that he was cold, but saw nothing that gave him away. I reached my Jeep and unlocked it.

"It was nice to meet you, Conrad. Maybe we'll see each other again soon."

He nodded, and I saw his gaze land on my neck.

"I know you're dying to ask." I pulled the collar of my jacket aside, so he could get a better look. "It's a dragon."

He leaned in closer, and I could feel his breath on my cheek, warming the spot in front of my ear. The movement was innocent, yet felt extremely intimate. I had to command myself to stay still. I battled between wanting to step back and longing to lean into him.

He pulled back just enough to look into my eyes. "It's amazing. Did it take long?"

I shrugged. "Not terribly."

He had no idea how amazing it really was. Supernatural residents and visitors had to register with the Court of the Sun and the Moon. We were each tagged with a magic tattoo that helped them keep track of anyone who broke the carefully constructed rules that made our town a true haven for us. Mine was designed by a friend and tattooed and magically infused by Addie, one of the official tattooists for the Court.

He stepped back to his former spot, which wasn't quite an arm's length away. Conrad reached for the inside of his right wrist and rubbed it absentmindedly, which wouldn't have been overly weird except he wore a large leather cuff over it. He was rubbing the cuff, and I wasn't sure he even realized he was doing it.

"So . . ." I attempted to divert the conversation to him. "Do you have any tattoos?"

He nodded. "I do. Quite a few actually." He pulled up one sleeve of his shirt, only to reveal another sleeve of the tattooed variety.

I gasped. "Holy shit, that's amazing."

I moved in for a closer look. Vines with thorns threaded their way around and through an intricate graveyard scene, complete with bones, tombstones, and heavy fog. In the distance a lone motorcycle sat near a large monument shaped like a cross. I reached for his arm and turned it to see the backside. In that moment, I felt him stiffen. I looked up into his eyes and noticed an intensity I'd never seen in anyone before. Heat seared my fingers where they touched his flesh. It wasn't your average attraction kind of warmth, but almost as if his veins were filled with hot magma. I couldn't let go. I didn't want to.

"Jetta," he whispered.

I straightened up slowly, still gripping his arm. That arm snaked around my waist and pulled me closer as my palms rested on his chest. My brain screamed at me to step back, that this was way too fast, despite my attraction to him. But my damn body wouldn't cooperate with my head. I melted into him, the extreme heat now flowing over every part of my body that touched his. It should have been uncomfortable, but I only wanted more.

He bent his head to mine, and our lips touched softly. It wasn't wild or passionate, as I'd expected a kiss from someone like him to be. Instead, the gesture was tender, filled with an emotion I wasn't sure either of us understood. When he pulled back, he looked just as confused as I felt.

"That was . . . nice." I struggled to find the correct words.

His eyes roamed my face for a brief moment, then he made a deep growling sound in the back of his throat and said, "I'm not even remotely nice."

His lips crashed down on mine, and the kiss I'd originally been expecting took over. His grip tightened as his tongue slipped between my lips. I opened for him, letting him explore and tease. I held fistfuls of his shirt as I tried to somehow pull him even closer than we already were. His large hands ran over my back as he pressed himself into me. This had to be what heaven felt like. Desire coursed through me, and I sank into the feeling just before logic forced its way through my lust-induced haze. I did not know this man. This was way too fast, even for me.

I pushed him away. "I'm sorry. I can't do this."

I turned and opened the door to my Jeep.

Conrad leaned his forearms on the top of my door. "Jetta, I apologize. I didn't mean to cross any lines." I looked up and his expression of contrition was genuine.

I shook my head as I took my place behind the steering wheel. "You didn't. I'm just not ready for something like this."

"Something like what?" he asked. "It was just a kiss."

"I don't know, Conrad. I just . . ." He was right, and I was probably overreacting, but I could have sworn there was something else happening while we kissed. I had no idea what that could have possibly been, and it made no sense. I couldn't think. Any words that came to mind were inadequate to describe the terror that pulled at my chest when I realized how lost I'd been while kissing him. It wasn't a danger kind of fear, but more of a warning signal. There was something happening on a spiritual level that I didn't understand.

I couldn't allow myself to lose control. Ever. Anyone that could fracture the carefully cultivated mastery of my emotions was someone to stay away from.

He had the potential to destroy me.

"I'm sorry. I need to go." I shut the door, jerking it out from underneath him. The gears protested as I slammed the Jeep in reverse and backed out of the parking spot. I refused to allow myself to even a peek in the rearview mirror.

I woke up in an unusually grumpy mood. I'd never been a morning person, but today I felt like terrorizing the village, so to speak. I needed to rein that in if I didn't want an incident on my hands. The Court had been lenient with me on past transgressions, thanks to my father, but I was running out of get-out-of-jail-free passes. Eventually they'd boot me out of town, and as much as I hated my father, I truly did love Havenwood Falls. My time away had only driven that point home all the more.

Lots of strong coffee was in order, so I grabbed a table at Coffee Haven and ordered the largest cup of coffee they sold. I was halfway through it when Zoey and her boyfriend Jordan walked through the door, hand in hand.

"Aunt Jetta!" Zoey skipped to my table, with Jordan in tow and trying to keep up.

"Hey, guys. Have a seat." I motioned to the chairs opposite mine.

"We can't stay. We just came to grab coffee before school." She looked at Jordan and smiled. "And since we saw you, we wanted to come say thank you."

"For what?" I asked, taking another sip of my coffee.

"For reminding us that we can make it through anything as long as we talk to each other honestly," replied Jordan.

"Ah, well . . . normally I'd not be the person to take relationship advice from, but I learned that tidbit from your parents." I directed my gaze at Zoey. "They're pretty smart when they aren't being stuffy."

She laughed. "Yeah, I guess you're right."

Jordan glanced at his watch. "We'd better grab our coffee and get going, or we'll be late for first period."

Zoey bent down for a hug and then waved goodbye as they made their way to the counter, still holding hands.

"Ah, young love. Isn't it sweet?" said a voice from behind me. I recognized that voice, and it set my teeth on edge.

"Hello, Bradly. What caused you to crawl out from under your rock?"

He stepped around my table and took a seat across from me. "You're so cheerful. I'm amazed the mayor hasn't named you citizen of the year."

"I'm amazed you haven't been named douche-nozzle of the year," I shot back.

"Tsk, tsk. Such language." His sardonic smile revealed a row of crooked, yellowed teeth.

I had a few choice words for him, but we were in public, so instead of sharing them, I said, "What do you want, Bradly?"

"Do I have to want something?"

"You always want something." I glared at him. "Spit it out."

"I heard you were in possession of something special. Something that might be of great interest to the right buyer."

My mind flashed to the lockbox under my bed at the inn. "I have no idea what you're talking about." I kept my face passive as I continued to sip my coffee.

"Oh, but I think you do." He winked at me. I generally loved the fae population, but Bradly was the rare exception. He was a dishonest and disreputable member of the Unseelie fae. I was amazed he had the gall to show his face in public after some of the stunts he'd pulled.

"Do you have something in your eye?" I asked when he winked a second time.

"What? No." He looked confused at my questioning. He wasn't exactly the sharpest crayon in the box.

"Would you like me to put something there?" I held up my spoon and pointed it at his face.

He shrank back. "Why are you always such a bitch?"

"Now who's using language?" I placed the spoon on the table, glanced around to assure we weren't drawing attention, and then leaned forward, looking him directly in his beady little black eyes. I felt my pupils constrict, and I knew they had changed to their reptilian form. "Don't ever try to pull me into your illicit activities again. I don't work for you or any of the Unseelie. You tricked me once, shame on you. Try to trick me twice . . ." I leaned back and stirred my coffee, letting my pupils regain their human shape. "Well, let's just say I've heard fae are a delicacy in some circles. I'd be happy to introduce you to those particular connoisseurs."

"You dare threaten the Unseelie?" he sputtered.

"No, I'm threatening you. Stay away from me. Stay away from my family. Stay away from my friends. If you don't, I'll be sure you disappear forever." I stood up and tossed my napkin on the table. "Goodbye, Bradly." I left him sitting there as I worked on calming my nerves.

I made the short walk from Coffee Haven to Simple Treasures Pawn Shop. Tristan was working, and I needed a distraction, and possibly some brotherly advice. I didn't foresee that distraction showing up in the form of Conrad. I walked into the shop only to run directly into him, my face colliding with his chest. His hand lurched out to steady me so I wouldn't fall. That same intense heat started at his fingers and traveled up my arm.

"Sorry," I blurted out quickly and stepped away.

He hooked his thumbs in his jean pockets.

"No need to apologize." He tilted his head slightly, and his gaze landed on my lips. I knew from the way he looked at me that he was thinking about that kiss, and to be honest, so was I.

I stepped aside. "It's good to see you again."

I hoped he'd take the hint and finish walking out the door. He didn't.

"Yeah, you too. Hey, since you're here, maybe you can help me with something." He smiled, and my heart jumped in my chest.

"Okay." Maybe if I kept it short and sweet, we could get this over with faster. I hated that he could reduce me to emotional tatters when just minutes ago I'd been handing out death threats with nerves of steel.

"I was in here shortly after I arrived in town and have been considering this ring." He led me over to the glass display counter and pointed to a silver ring with a Celtic emblem on it.

I squatted down for a better look.

"And?" I asked, with a bit more impatience than I'd intended.

"What do you think? Do you know anything about the symbolism?" He crouched down next to me.

I closed my eyes a moment and tried to focus on anything other than his cologne, which was spicy and a little smoky. That scent assaulted my senses in ways I did not want to experience.

"Not really. It looks Celtic. That's about all I can tell you." I stood and stepped back from the counter.

He followed me up and put his hands in his pockets. "Yeah, that's about all anyone seems to know."

"Jetta! So glad you finally came by to see me." My brother Tristan emerged from the back room with a large book in his hand. He glanced between us. "I see you've met Conrad."

I nodded. "Yeah, he was at my set last night."

Tristan smiled. "She's very talented. And neglectful." He turned to face me directly. "Bianca is furious with you for skipping town without keeping in touch. She's insisting you join us for dinner tonight."

I cringed. "So sorry. I owe you all some explanations. What time? Six?"

Tristan nodded. "Hey, Conrad, you should join us as well. We could finish discussing some of those historical ruins we'd been talking about. I think I found more in this book."

I felt my eyes bulge out of their sockets. If it were physically possible for them to jump from my head, I think they would have bounced all over the room. Why the hell was Tristan inviting this stranger to his home?

Conrad glanced at me, then back at Tristan. "I'm not sure—"

Tristan interrupted. "I insist."

He didn't even glance my way. He just kept smiling at Conrad like he was some kind of visiting dignitary. *Idiot brother.*

"I'd be honored," Conrad answered, as his gaze quickly flickered from Tristan's face to mine once more.

"Yeah, that'd be great," I muttered with exactly zero enthusiasm.

CHAPTER 8

CONRAD

I sat on my bed at the inn and stared at the photo of Jetta. She'd changed her appearance quite a bit from her time in Georgia, but there was no mistaking I was looking at the same woman. I hadn't yet figured out how I was getting her back to Atlanta, but I hoped tonight's dinner would move me closer to an answer. Jetta was quite a woman. Strong, independent, rebellious. She appeared to know what she wanted and how she planned to achieve it. And damn it all—the more I was with her, the more I wanted her for myself.

This was a new experience for me. But in truth, all I could do was enjoy her company, learn everything I could, and hope this entire situation would have a peaceful resolution for everyone involved. I still needed to figure out where she'd hidden the lockbox she'd taken, but that might be something I'd have to deal with once I'd revealed my purpose here. I still held on to hope that I could convince her to trust me. I'd only known her a short time, but she'd already made that plan hard to execute.

I turned on my phone to check messages, and the screen informed me I had missed ten calls from Brandt. I groaned. "Son of a bitch. Give me time, asshole."

I pushed the button to call him back and half hoped it wouldn't go through. It did.

"Monroe! Why the hell haven't you been taking my calls?" yelled Brandt's voice.

"I'm in a canyon. Reception sucks and only works on rare occasion." I knew he heard the exhaustion in my voice. I was tired. Of him.

"Do you have any updates for me?" His voice was calmer now.

"I do." I hesitated. I wasn't ready to divulge everything, so decided to be vague. "I think I've found her. If I can verify it's her, I'll take the next step," I lied.

Her identity was not in question, but I still held my reservations on how much to involve him. Knowing Brandt's type, he'd send his goons down to help and screw it all up. I needed to keep him in the dark until I was almost there.

"Well . . . that's something anyway." He huffed and sounded like a spoiled teen.

"This kind of thing takes a little time, but I will deliver. Just hang on until I can be sure I've got everything you need taken care of." I hoped my reassurances would get him off my back for a while.

"I'd appreciate frequent updates," he said, adding, "when you have cell service."

"When I can." I hung up.

The more I talked to him, the less I liked him. And that was saying a lot, considering I didn't like him to begin with.

I buttoned up my blue dress shirt, leaving my sleeves rolled halfway up my forearms. I didn't own slacks, but I'd felt certain the Mills family weren't that formal, so my best pair of jeans would be fine. Once ready, I hurried to my truck, surprised at how anxious I was for the evening to start. I could have pretended it wasn't because I was seeing Jetta again, but that would only have been lying to myself. I was very attracted to her, and while it wasn't wise, I was enjoying this self-torture more than I should have.

I studied the small map Tristan had drawn for me. Havenwood Falls was a cozy little town, easily traveled from one side to the other in minutes. Finding Tristan's home was easy, and I'd arrived with time to spare. Tristan lived in a nice house. Better than anything I can ever remember calling home. The ranch-style brick layout looked spacious, even from the outside. I stepped out of my truck and turned to see Jetta pulling in behind me. She wasted no time getting out of her Jeep and confronting me.

"Why are you here?" Her voice held every bit of the suspicion her words did.

"Dinner," I said, as I held up a bottle of wine I'd picked up for Tristan's wife Bianca. "Everyone I asked said Stone Falls was the place to buy a good bottle of Pinot. Were they right?"

She took a step closer, her eyes boring into mine. "Don't try to change the subject. What are you up to?"

I put one hand on my hip.

"My, if we aren't a little paranoid," I said defensively. She was getting too close to finding me out, and I couldn't allow that yet. I pushed down the urge to blurt the truth out and be done with it.

"I . . ." She balled up her fists. "I have good reason to be." She grabbed my shirt collar and pulled me to her, nose to nose. "If you have even the smallest hint of nefarious intentions toward my family, I will end you." She shoved me away and stomped into the house.

"Well," I muttered to myself. "This should be fun."

TRISTAN POURED a second glass of wine and offered some to Jetta.

"No, thanks. I've had two glasses already," she said.

She'd been quiet all evening, and that obviously wasn't her normal modus operandi when in a family setting. Zoey had chatted excitedly off and on throughout the meal, the subjects ranging from school to the latest fashion trends. I listened attentively and smiled in what I assumed were all the right places. She was a sweet kid, and her enthusiasm for subjects she loved was infectious. She helped fill the awkward silences anytime the conversation included Jetta, whose replies were short and indifferent.

Bianca stood, gathering dishes. "Jetta, would you help me in the kitchen?"

Jetta nodded and stood, picking up her dishes and scooping up Zoey's as she passed.

Tristan motioned for me to join him on the sofa. The living room, dining room, and kitchen were all connected in one large open floor plan. I glanced toward the back of the room, where Jetta, Zoey, and Bianca had gathered around the sink.

"Shouldn't we help with the cleanup?" I'd always hated the idea that the kitchen was "women's work."

"Normally, I'd say yes, but that request to Jetta was code for 'let's talk in private.' No way I'm interrupting that." Tristan chuckled. "I value my life too much."

I understood. "You have an amazing family, Tristan. You're a lucky man."

I meant every word. I'd never had a family, even as a child. He was blessed with something I hoped he didn't take for granted.

"I am indeed. Those three women in there are the center of my world." He opened the book he'd brought from the pawn shop. "I found something interesting."

I sat next to him, both of us now facing the fireplace on the opposite end of the room, our backs to the kitchen. Tristan placed the book in my lap, opened to a specific page. A Celtic triskele rested above the description of its meaning. Below that were several paragraphs explaining variations of the symbols that had been found over the years.

"I ran across something vague, but it might explain that ring you were talking about. It also may have a connection to the ruins in the Andes mountain range that we'd discussed."

"Those are connected?" I couldn't believe my ears. The subject of the ruins had only come up because I'd noticed a painting in the pawn shop, and it reminded me of a favorite book I'd had as a child. I couldn't even remember the name of it. I just recalled being fascinated with the chapters on volcanoes, ruins, and mountains in South America. Odd how that book was one of the few memories I had of my childhood. "What a weird coincidence."

Tristan smiled. "I don't think it's a coincidence at all."

"You don't believe in coincidences?" I asked.

He shook his head. "Not in Havenwood Falls."

My eyebrows drew together in confusion.

"Hey, guys," Bianca interrupted. "How about we start a fire?"

"Sounds good. I'll grab some wood from the bin." Tristan moved to stand, but I stopped him.

"Please, allow me. It's the least I can do for such an amazing meal."

Bianca smiled. "That'd be very kind of you."

Tristan pointed to the back door that led from the kitchen. "There's a small shed just outside that door. You'll find plenty of firewood in there."

"Great, I'll be right back." I was happy for the excuse to get some fresh air. My head was spinning from the odd bit of information Tristan had given me. How did my tattoo and South American ruins connect?

I shut the kitchen door behind me and inhaled sharply. Havenwood Falls had clean, crisp air, and I greatly appreciated that. Even the air in the bars was less stale and putrid. I allowed myself another deep breath, and then I walked to the shed. The door was unlatched and slightly ajar. With caution, I slowly opened it. Then the smell of whiskey hit me, mixed with a floral scent that I instantly recognized as Jetta's.

I leaned against the door jamb and crossed my arms. "Do you always sneak drinks in the woodshed?"

She jumped. "Damn you. You scared the hell out of me."

"Maybe you shouldn't be skulking in your brother's backyard."

"I'm not . . ." She put her thumb to her temple and rubbed it. "I needed a break."

"So your idea of a break is hiding in the dark, drinking whiskey, surrounded by dead trees. Lovely. I now know what to get you for Christmas."

"You're an asshole." She threw back the last of her drink and sat the cup on a small pile of wood near the door.

I entered, blocking her only exit. "You know what I think?"

She shook her head. "I don't care what you think."

I ignored her. "I think you're out here because you're avoiding me."

She huffed. "Don't flatter yourself."

"I'm just stating facts." I continued to smile at her. She was so fun to rile up.

"You are in my way. Move." She put her hands out to physically move me, then thought better of it. "Please."

I couldn't help it. I had to push her buttons. "So, you're not scared of me at all."

"Not a bit," she countered.

"Then move me." I stood my ground.

"What? That's stupid. Just step back and let me by." She glared at me.

Instead of stepping back, I stepped closer to her.

"Wrong way, moron." She reached out and pushed me back one step.

I felt her tense up as her hands lingered on my chest. In the next moment, I had her back against the wall, my arms on either side of her shoulders.

"Why are you fighting this?" I whispered.

She looked up at me, and her hands slowly lowered to her sides. "I'm not fighting anything."

Her eyes were focused on my chin.

"Can you look me in the eye and tell me you don't feel anything between us?" I stared down at her.

She raised her eyes to mine and took in a shaky breath. "No."

Her hands slid up my chest, and she hooked them behind my neck. I stepped closer, and she pulled me down to her.

When my lips met hers, a rush of electricity pulsed through me. My blood heated, and my skin became over-sensitized. Every touch made me crazier than the one before. I wanted to be closer to her. I needed to be a part of her in every way.

I slid my hands to her ass and squeezed. She pulled herself up, wrapping her legs around my waist. I pressed her into the wall and ground against her. I was consumed by my need for her.

She reached a hand between us and slid it down my stomach. Once she reached my waistband, I felt her pop the button of my jeans. I groaned into her mouth as I felt the jerky movements of her fingers working my zipper.

"Aunt Jetta? Are you out here?" Zoey's voice drifted through the doorway.

Jetta gasped and pushed me away. "Oh no." She hissed. "Zip your pants up. Hurry." She worked to straighten her clothes.

I turned my back to the door and quickly buttoned my jeans.

"Damn it," I muttered.

"Uh, yeah. I'm in here." Jetta glanced at me quickly to be sure I was decent.

The door swung open wide, and Zoey stood on the other side.

"Hey, sweetie," Jetta said. "We're just, uh . . ."

"Getting wood for the fire." I turned to Jetta. "Do you think one armload is enough? Or should we both grab a load?"

"Our fireplace is big, but it isn't that big," laughed Zoey.

"Good point, short stuff. Two loads would be overkill." Jetta pulled her into a quick hug. "Let's let Conrad handle that, and we'll go find the cake your mom made."

I grabbed a stack of wood and followed them into the house.

CHAPTER 9

JETTA

I kept my distance from Conrad the rest of the evening. We'd almost made a huge mistake. Despite my attraction, I didn't trust him. He'd shown up out of nowhere and within days had integrated himself into our lives. I didn't know why Simon and Tristan seemed to like him so much, but I refused to let my guard down. I'd never claimed to be a romantic. And while I could understand lust easily enough, when Conrad kissed me, it felt like he'd been expecting so much more than I was willing to give. More than I was *able* to give.

He was human. And even if I were to decide I wanted a soul mate, I didn't think it would ever work. I adored the humans in my life. My sister-in-law was a blessing from above. Jordan made Zoey extremely happy. But I didn't think I had what it took to spend my life with another person, dragon or otherwise. Not to mention that my instincts told me something wasn't quite on the level where Conrad was concerned. But my instincts hadn't always been correct. Could I have been so wrong about Conrad? Was I denying myself his touch simply because I'd had a few bad experiences?

I excused myself early and went back to the inn. Visions of my encounter with Conrad played on repeat in my head. I didn't want to think about him. I needed to rid myself of this odd obsession, so a friendship with him would be possible and a relationship wouldn't be tempting. At least then I wouldn't be on high alert every time I saw him. But I was worrying for nothing, right? He was only here for a short time.

I approached my room and noticed my door was slightly cracked. I knew I'd locked up behind me. Panic ripped through my chest as I entered the room and found it had been ransacked.

I went straight to the bed and flipped up the mattress. It landed with a thud against the opposite wall. The lockbox was gone.

"Damn it all to hell!" I shouted.

I slammed the door shut behind me as I stomped down the stairs and into the lobby. Sindi had just hung up the phone as I reached the check-in desk.

"Have you seen that little squid-faced pile of shit in here tonight?" I asked.

Sindi's brow raised. "You'll have to be more specific. I know a few who fit that description."

"Bradly Russo." I put my hands on my hips and tapped my foot with impatience. I needed to find him fast.

"Oh, that little squid-faced pile of shit. Yeah, he was here not twenty minutes ago." She pointed to the door. "He left, heading toward the square."

"Thanks." I ran out the door and looked around. A few people milled about the square, but the hour was late enough that most of the normal nighttime crowds had thinned out.

"Looking for someone?" Conrad's voice was amused.

"You have a talent for knowing the worst possible time to talk to me," I muttered. "Why aren't you still at my brother's?" I continued to scan the area, hoping to catch a glimpse of Bradly.

He shrugged. "I was worried about you. We didn't get to talk after making out, and I wanted to be sure you were okay."

I rolled my eyes. "Why do men assume that women are so fragile that they can't handle their emotions after sex?"

"I never said that. I said I wanted to be sure you were okay. You seemed pretty mad at me." He grimaced. "And we didn't have sex, although I'm still up for it, if you are."

"I don't really have time for this right now." I ran across the street to the square, trying to determine which way Bradly might have gone.

Conrad's heavy steps were right behind me. "What are you looking for?"

I ran my hands through my hair in frustration. "Someone stole something from me. I know who did it, and I need to find him. Now."

Conrad's face changed from amusement to concern. "What did he take?"

"A lockbox," I said. "It had some family heirlooms in it. I can't lose them."

He nodded. "How can I help?"

I frowned. The last thing I wanted was to owe Conrad, but we could cover more ground quicker if we split up. "You take the south side of the square and then the west. I'll take the east side and move to the north. We'll meet on the corner. Ask people if they've seen Bradly Russo, and if so, which way he went. They'll know who you mean."

He nodded. "One problem."

"What?" I sighed.

"I don't know who he is. I might walk right past him." Conrad had a point.

"You can't miss him. Dark hair, beady eyes, short and plump. He looks like a pale Oompa Loompa."

"Wow, that's quite a description," he said.

"It's mostly accurate," I replied.

"Okay then, see you at the corner."

Conrad followed Main Street as I made my way up Eleventh. I peeked my head between buildings and in doorways, hoping someone had seen him, or that I would spot him. Nothing. Once I reached City Hall, I ran into an elderly man I'd seen a time or two at Coffee Haven. I couldn't remember his name, but he'd always been friendly.

"Hi." I approached him. "Would you happen to have seen a friend of mine? He's short, dark hair and eyes, kinda round—"

The man nodded. "Yeah, I just saw a guy like that running up Eighth Street with a box in his hands."

"Thank you!" I shouted as I sprinted toward Eighth. Conrad must have seen me running because he followed me. I ran almost three blocks before realizing I was near Havenwood Heights.

"Fuck!" I kicked a tree and shouted again. "Son of a bitch."

Conrad jogged up behind me, only slightly out of breath. "Did you see him?"

"No. I was told he went this way." I looked around and then remembered that Bradly used to have a small shack out in the wooded area that stood between the back of Sun and Moon Academy and Alverson Road. "I think I know where he is."

I jogged back the way we'd come, pacing myself a little better than the first time. I needed to reach my Jeep and find his place before he figured out a way to open the lockbox.

Conrad kept up, and when we reached my Jeep, he climbed in the passenger seat.

"Really, you don't need to help," I said.

"I want to. I promise not to put my hands on you."

I glanced at him with skepticism.

He grinned. "Or my lips. Or any other part of my body."

I felt a smirk coming on. It wouldn't help my cause if he realized he could make me laugh. I cleared my throat and started the car. "Fine."

I backed out and hauled ass across Main until I hit Fourth, then drove north until Fourth became Alverson Road. As we neared the edge of town, Conrad spoke up.

"So, what's in this box that's so important?" he asked.

"I told you, family stuff." I pulled into a small cutout near some trees and cut the engine.

"What kind of family stuff?" He was annoyingly curious.

"A salad shooter," I said and hopped out of the car.

"A what?" His voice held disbelief.

"Haven't you ever seen a salad shooter?" I asked. "They're hard to find, and this one is special." I knew he heard the sarcasm in my voice.

"What, was this one passed down from Thomas Edison?" He crossed his arms as he approached me.

"Exactly. He invented them." I was no longer paying attention to him. I was mentally plotting out the land and trying to remember exactly where that little weasel's hideout was.

I glanced at Conrad, who now stood at the edge of the tree line, looking into the dark expanse of the forest. I needed to shift. Making good time was critical. I also had a better chance of spotting the shack from the air.

"Hey, Conrad, would you mind looking in the back of my Jeep for some flashlights? I'm pretty sure I have some in there somewhere. We don't want to head out into that copse of trees without them."

He nodded and jogged to the door. Once he'd crawled in back, I took off at a run. I didn't have time to undress, and for a brief moment, Zoey's idea of Velcro clothes came to mind. Maybe she was on to something there. I allowed myself to shift as I ran, my clothes tearing from my body and falling to the forest floor. Being naked later would suck, but I'd worry about that when the time came.

I remembered there was a small clearing up ahead, so I pushed my way through and then stretched my wings. With a few powerful flaps, I was high in the air. Activating my camouflage, I started circling the area, diving here and there to move in for a closer look as I expanded my radius. For a few minutes, all I saw were trees. My vision wasn't as sharp at night, so I was having to move slower than I liked to.

Then I saw and smelled a small trail of smoke coming from what appeared to be leaves and branches. It had to be Bradly. I made a light landing and slowly pushed my way to the spot where his shack was hidden. He'd covered the roof to match the forest floor, and if it hadn't been for the fireplace, I probably would have missed it.

I shifted back to my human form and crept to the door. I listened but could only hear light humming. It sounded as if he were alone. That would sure make it easier.

I glanced down at my naked body. "Well, Bradly, get ready for a thrill. It might be the last thing you ever see," I whispered.

I pulled the door open slightly, trying to be as quiet as possible. The candles and glow of the small fireplace gave off a dim light. Bradly had his back to the door and was bent over a small table. His humming was off-key as he fidgeted with whatever was in front of him. I could only assume he was working on my lockbox, or rather, Brandt's lockbox.

One glance around the room revealed that he spent a lot of time there. Rickety wood walls were lined with shelves containing pots, pans, canned goods, and dishes. A small mattress was nestled in one corner of the room, blankets thrown haphazardly on top. Dirt covered every inch of the floor, and I couldn't tell if it was truly a dirt floor, or if he was just a disgusting pig. My money was on pig. The beat-up wooden table he worked at sat in the middle of the room.

All dragons had a special gift, and mine was stealth. It helped me in both my human and dragon forms. A light step allowed me to sneak in and out of my father's house many times as a teen. My ninja-like gifts had made me popular with the seedy crowd, such as Bradly and his ilk, when I'd been dumb enough to lend my services. Since fae possessed keen senses, I relied heavily on that gift now as I snuck inside the shack.

I tiptoed behind Bradly until I was only a couple of feet away.

His head popped up, and he stopped singing. He sniffed the air, his body appearing stiff and on alert.

"Hey, asswipe, that doesn't belong to you."

He gasped and turned around, the lockbox clutched firmly in his hands. Then he looked at me and dropped it on the ground. I let him take in an eyeful. It wouldn't matter what he saw once I'd fed him to one of my friends—or ate him myself. That thought almost made me gag. Friends it was.

"Uh . . . how'd you . . ." He gawked, staring at my womanly body parts. Parts he'd probably only ever seen in pictures. "You're naked."

"Yep, and you're dead." I stepped forward, and he lunged for the box, landing on top of it. I grabbed him and held him up in the air, the box dangling from his fingers.

"Let go, and I might have mercy on you."

He gasped and twisted, trying to wrench free. "No, I need the ring!"

"What?" I asked.

"You wouldn't let me finish telling you. I need the ring! I want out of this town. I can't be followed." He grunted as I dropped him.

"That's all you wanted?" I asked, still not sure I believed him. "How do you know there is a ring?"

He rubbed his lower back and stood up. "Because Ani told me about it. She said she gave you a ring, so you could leave town without a trace."

I glowered at him. "Ani should really keep her mouth shut. If the Court finds out about her shenanigans, they'll string her up by her toes."

Bradly nodded, then resumed staring at my naked torso.

"Do you have a blanket or something I can cover up with?"

He shook his head.

"Fine, give me the damn box."

He handed it to me, and I turned from his view. I punched in the code and heard the lid click open. When I turned back around, I found he'd been staring at my ass.

I held the ring out to him. "Here, take it." I snapped the box shut. "But if you ever tell anyone where it came from, I will deny it. It'll be your and Ani's word against mine. I'm not the town saint, but they'll all believe me before they believe you, got it?"

He nodded.

"Great, now I don't ever want to see your grubby little face again."

I turned—to see Conrad standing in the doorway. His jaw hung open, and his eyes shifted from me to Bradly, then to me again.

"Oh, dear goddess," I groaned. This just became way worse.

He held my shredded clothes in his hands. "What the hell happened?" He glanced at Bradly. "Are you having sex with this troll? Is this why you keep shutting me out?"

"Hey now, there's no need to be nasty." Bradly bristled.

The very idea. I started laughing. I know I should have been embarrassed and angry, but goddess help me, I started laughing.

Conrad looked at me like I was a lunatic, which made me laugh even more. Behind me, Bradly released a nervous laugh, and Conrad shot him a look that could have turned him to stone.

Bradly stopped his laughter abruptly and said, "I need to get out of town. Now. Please leave."

"My, we are in a hurry," I drawled. "What did you do this time?"

"Nothing. Go away." His face pinched together in frustration.

I shrugged as I turned and walked toward Conrad. The lockbox was in my hand as my other reached for the clothes he held. Once I'd stepped outside the door, I sat the box on a stump and examined what remained of my jeans and sweater.

Conrad stood behind me, and I could feel his eyes on me. The urge to laugh faded, and now I was acutely aware of his nearness. Of the fact that I was naked in front of the man I so desperately wanted but should never touch.

His warm hand brushed the back of my neck, and I froze, unsure of his next move. I felt his breath for a brief moment, then his lips touched the spot where my spine and shoulders met. His warmth spread through me, and I closed my eyes. Then his jacket was placed around me.

"Zip it up," he ordered.

I turned to face him, my emotions in turmoil as I followed his command. He handed me the lockbox, then looked down at my bare legs and feet. "I'm not gonna ask right now, but I will eventually."

Then without another word he picked me up and carried me out of the forest.

CHAPTER 10

CONRAD

I needed a stiff drink and a very cold shower. I had no idea what the hell I'd stumbled upon in the forest, but it would take a hell of a lot of booze to erase it from my mind. No, scratch that. I'd go to my grave with the vision of Jetta's gorgeous body engraved in my brain. It wasn't fair for a woman to be that alluring. The need for her was already suffocating me, and seeing her naked only intensified that desire to claim her.

"This is not going as planned," I muttered under my breath as I drove us back to the inn.

"What was that?" Jetta asked from the passenger side of the Jeep. Her long, shapely legs were tucked under her as she leaned against the door.

"Nothing. I'm just tired." I glanced at her. "It's been a weird day."

She nodded. "You're telling me."

I found a parking spot and turned off the ignition. "Why are you staying here, instead of at your house?"

It frustrated me to know we'd been staying at the same inn since arriving in town and I'd missed it. I must have been losing my touch.

She stretched for a moment, and I caught a glimpse of her thighs. "My dad and I hate each other. I can't stay there anymore."

I nodded in understanding. "You don't have your own place?"

"Not at the moment. I refuse to buy anything with Daddy's money.

When I buy a house, I want it to be something I've earned." She opened the door and stepped out, taking the lockbox with her.

I exited as well and walked around to her side of the Jeep. "Do you think you're decent enough to walk into the lobby?"

She looked down at the jacket that hit just below the top of her thighs. "Close enough."

I motioned for her to lead the way. "Age before beauty."

She snorted. "You have no idea."

We stepped into the blissfully empty lobby. She hurried up the stairs, and I was only a few steps behind her, trying not to look but enjoying the view as the hem of the jacket rose and fell with each step.

We reached her room, and I gauged its distance from mine. There were only seven rooms on the second floor, and I was at the end of the hall, so the walk to my door would take less than a few seconds. I gave myself a mental shake. No matter what I saw or what we'd done so far, she was still closing me off. Not just sexually, but even personal discussions were off limits. I needed to remove the intimacy idea from my mind. Besides, that's not what I came here to do. Not exactly anyway.

"Well, good night, Jetta," I said softly, before pulling out the key to my own room.

She put her hand on my arm and stepped closer. "Thank you, Conrad. You went above and beyond tonight. I appreciate it." She tilted up on her toes and gently pressed her lips to mine.

I studied her face as she pulled back, and she gave me a genuine smile. Something stabbed at my heart.

"Anytime." I walked to my end of the hall, and just as I unlocked my door, I turned to see her watching me from her own doorway. I smiled at her. "By the way, that dream-catcher tattoo on your hip is pretty hot."

Her mouth popped open, then shut just as quickly. I chuckled as I closed my own door.

MY DREAMS WERE FILLED with images of Jetta. Naked. Not that I hadn't imagined her that way before, but the truth was so much better than my imagination. I'd spent the morning trying to think of anything but her, which was difficult since she was the reason I was there. I now knew she had the box, but getting it from her could be tricky. If I could convince her to give it back, maybe Brandt would be content enough to let her punishment slide. But last night proved Jetta was willing to do whatever it took to keep the items she'd stolen. There wasn't anything about completing this job that was going to be easy.

I parked my truck down the street and watched her Jeep. Once she left, I could break into her room and grab the box. Then I'd try to negotiate with Brandt. With any luck, she'd be left out of it completely. Brandt would recover his belongings, and Jetta would never know what happened. I was being selfish, but I didn't want her to ever learn the truth of my visit to Havenwood Falls. I'd like to leave her on good terms. I wasn't sure why that really mattered to me, but it did. If Brandt couldn't accept that outcome, well . . . I'd received my twenty-five thousand. I'd just have to make that work. I wasn't going to force her to do anything she didn't want to do, including going back to Atlanta.

By noon, I was about to give up on the idea that she might leave her room. Just as I'd started to work out a new plan, I saw her exit the inn, with the box under her arm. *Shit.*

She pulled away in her Jeep, and I did my best to follow at a discreet distance. Once we left the residential areas behind, I became suspicious.

She pulled up to a small trail and parked at the entrance. I hung back so she wouldn't notice me. I watched as she stepped out of the Jeep with the box and started up the trail. I pulled over enough that I wouldn't be in the road, then I parked and jogged to the footpath she'd just entered.

Jetta hiked her way up the pathway, stopping occasionally to adjust her hold on the box. Then she veered off the well-used trail and tromped through the dense trees. I struggled to stay quiet now that I had branches and leaves underfoot instead of a dirt road. I moved slowly, keeping her in sight as much as possible without getting too close.

After about fifteen minutes, she'd arrived at a beautiful little lake with a small waterfall at one edge. I held my breath as I witnessed her walk the treacherous looking stone steps to the edge of the falls. She adjusted the box once more, then stepped forward and disappeared into a dark cavern.

I frowned. She didn't just disappear into the darkness. It's more like she was swallowed by it.

I took cautious steps as I neared the stairs. Once there, I realized they were actually wide and sturdy. I moved slowly, giving myself a moment to pause before advancing to the next step. As I moved closer, the stone surface became shiny from the mist coming off the waterfall. At the last step, I looked around for a good hiding place, should I need it. I saw a narrow indention behind some foliage and decided that would have to do in a pinch.

The mouth of the cave was incredibly dark. More so than seemed possible. I stepped around the corner and into the darkness. From the outside, the cave seemed small, but once I passed what could only be properly described as a veil of endless midnight, the space grew substantially. It was impossible, yet there was more light in the back of the cave than there was at the entrance.

I listened for Jetta but heard nothing. I stayed close to the outer wall as I took my time inching toward the back. I neared another small doorway and froze. I could hear someone moving around. I slowly poked my head around the door and caught a glimpse of a shimmering dirt wall before everything went black.

My head throbbed as if someone were using it as a bass drum. The sunshine above temporarily blinded me. I reached for my forehead and winced at the large knot above my left eyebrow. Once my vision cleared and the world stopped spinning around me, I managed to pull myself up into a sitting position. I'd been laid out flat on the bank next to the partially frozen waterfall. Jetta sat on a log at the edge of the tree line, watching me.

"Why are you following me?" Her expression was pure anger.

"It's a long story," I said.

She crossed her arms. "I have time."

I needed to think of something quick. "I was worried about that creepy troll guy getting to you."

She raised one eyebrow. "I don't think so."

"You don't?" I had no idea where to take my lie from there.

"No." She stood and then crouched down in front of me. Her eyes searched mine. "How did you get into my cave?"

"Uh . . ." I was the one hit on the head, so why was she asking the stupid question? "I walked in."

"How?" she asked again.

I looked down at my legs, wondering if I'd somehow overlooked an inability to use them that I didn't know about.

"With my legs," I replied slowly.

She stood and paced. "That's not what I mean."

"I have no idea what you're asking me, then." I tried to stand, but I was still a bit wobbly on my feet and needed a nearby tree to steady me. "What the hell did you hit me with?"

"A shovel," she said absentmindedly, then turned and looked me in the eyes again, as if she were trying to drive a point home. "Only very specific people can enter that cave. Very specific." She stared at me as if she were waiting for something. "Are you going to tell me your secret? It's not like I don't already know."

I felt my throat close. *She knows I'm after the box? After her?* "Listen, it wasn't my intention to deceive you. I was going to tell you the whole truth once I figured things out."

"Why does everyone say that *after* they are caught lying?" She still watched me closely.

"I couldn't tell you, yet." I didn't know how to explain my feelings and all that had happened over the last three days. Had it really only been three days? It felt like I'd known her forever.

She let out a harsh laugh. "This is Havenwood Falls, Conrad. People like us, we don't have to hide from each other. It's safe here."

"People like us?" I asked. Now I was really lost.

"Oh, you stubborn man." She kicked a fallen branch. "What clan did you originate from?"

"Clan?" I asked again.

"Are you a parrot? Why do you keep repeating my questions?"

"Because they aren't making any damn sense," I shot back, pain in my head stirring up my irritation.

"This." She pointed to the tattoo on her neck.

"Your dragon tattoo," I said.

She nodded.

I shrugged, still clueless.

"Only dragons can enter that cave!" she shouted as she pointed in the direction of the falls.

"Dragons? What is that, some kind of club?" I stretched my back, feeling every spot that had been stabbed by rocks and twigs as I lay on the forest floor.

She stepped closer and took my hand. The friction that existed between us flared to life. "I'm one too, Conrad. It's okay."

I was really getting tired of this odd conversation. "One what?"

"A dragon, just like you."

CHAPTER 11

JETTA

*D*amn, this man was thick. Didn't he realize he was surrounded by the supernatural? Didn't he realize he was safe here? It all made sense. Why he clicked with Simon and Tristan instantly. Why he and I had such chemistry. He wasn't a frost dragon, but he was a dragon shifter of some kind. There's no way he could have walked into my cave otherwise. The warding only allowed dragons to enter.

I looked up at his handsome and somewhat battered face. *Oops.* I probably shouldn't have beaned him with the shovel. I'd just finished digging a hole for the lockbox when he'd surprised me. Already in my hand, it made a convenient weapon, so that's how he ended up unconscious on the ground moments later.

I'd made sure I hadn't killed him, then I quickly buried the box. After assuring my secrets were well out of reach of anyone who might want them, I dragged him outside and waited for him to come around. Thankfully, it hadn't taken too long.

I motioned to his head. "I should probably take you to Zoey. She can help with that nasty bump."

"Your teenage niece?" He rubbed the area lightly, and I could see it hurt, even if he was trying to pretend it didn't. "Did she graduate from medical school as a prodigy or something?"

I laughed. "No, it's her tears. That's her gift."

I assumed he knew about dragons having special gifts. Zoey's happened to be that her tears could heal. Her gifts were amazing, but also dangerous. Only other dragons were allowed to know of her ability, as there were many supernaturals that would seek to harvest her for such a powerful endowment.

"Her tears," he repeated. He stepped closer to me, finally having regained his balance. "Are you on drugs or something? I know pot is legal here. How much have you had?"

"I don't smoke pot." I'd tried it once, but, just like alcohol, it didn't do much for dragons unless consumed in large quantities.

"Well, you're on something, because nothing you've said since I woke up is logical."

I frowned. Did I hit him too hard? I gasped. What if I'd damaged his brain and now he couldn't remember everything? *Shit.*

"Never mind. Let's get you home and have a doctor look at that head." I needed to talk to Tristan and find out what to do from there. I had to be sure I hadn't damaged him permanently.

I put my arm around him, and he leaned into me slightly. "Are you gonna be okay to walk?"

He nodded. "I think so."

He wobbled a moment.

"I'll help you, just in case."

He muttered something under his breath, but I didn't catch it. I chose to ignore him and focus on getting him back to the trail where there were fewer obstacles to trip over. It took longer than it normally should, but thankfully it was still early afternoon and we had no reason to rush. This part of the mountain wasn't always the safest place to be at night, even for dragons.

I helped him settle in to the passenger seat, then I held out my hand. "Keys."

"What? Why?" he asked.

"So I can move your truck over here where it's not near the road. It'll get sideswiped if we don't move it."

He shook his head. "Nah, it's okay. Just leave it."

I frowned. "It'll only take a couple of minutes. Give me the damn keys."

"Just take me to the doctor. The truck is fine."

I narrowed my eyes at him. "Why don't you want me in your truck?"

He sighed. "I just want to get my head looked at, okay?"

Guilt forced me to give up. He was suffering because of my actions, although to be fair, he shouldn't have been stalking me.

I sat in the driver's seat and turned the engine over. Trees flew by as we sped back into town. I didn't know the first thing about amnesia, but I figured the sooner he received care, the better.

"WHAT DO YOU THINK, TRISTAN?" I asked. I'd been pacing in the living room, my hands sore from wringing them as I walked.

"I think it's an odd situation," he stated.

"Odd how?"

"He doesn't recall his childhood at all, except a few things here and there. He says he was orphaned and doesn't have any living family. But I believe you're right, Jetta. He's a dragon shifter. I'm just not sure he remembers it."

"Oh no. I didn't mean to hit him that hard."

"I'm not convinced it was you," Tristan replied. "He'd told me about being orphaned the first day I met him. We'd discussed some ruins in Peru that he'd been infatuated with as a child, which led to us talking about childhood in general. He hadn't fully opened up, but he had told me his family was all gone."

I glanced at the spare bedroom Conrad was currently resting in.

Tristan motioned for me to follow him, and he pulled a book from one of his shelves. The same book he and Conrad had been poring over the night before. "That symbol Conrad was so interested in is here."

I recognized the triskele. It matched the ring in the pawn shop, with the exception that this one was comprised of jagged black lines.

"It turns out some clans added their own personal touches to these to represent their family line. I've seen a lot of varieties. The fire represents lava dragons."

I took a moment to roll the info around in my head. "So, Conrad is a lava dragon?"

Tristan shrugged. "That's my guess."

"But he doesn't remember it," I stated.

"Again, just my guess."

"Wow. This is heavy." I wasn't sure how to process it all. "Wait, how can he not know? Wouldn't he have shifted a few times?"

"Yeah," Tristan said, "there is that." He glanced at me, and his brows drew together. "What if he has something on him that prevents him from shifting?" He nodded at my neck. "We have magic infused tattoos. Maybe he has something similar?"

That made sense. He did have a lot of tattoos. It could be any one of them. Or maybe a piece of jewelry.

"It just seems so crazy that he wouldn't have a clue. When I mentioned dragons, he looked at me like I'd lost my mind."

"As far as he's concerned, dragons are just fantasy creatures in books and movies." Tristan ran a hand through his hair.

"So, what do we do?" I wasn't good with delicate situations. And while I wouldn't label Conrad as delicate, this whole secret dragon thing would have to be handled carefully.

"I think for now we go on as if we know only as much as he does. Play it by ear until we see the need to change that strategy."

The door to the guest room opened, and Conrad walked out. The knot on his head had started to turn a sickly yellowish-green. *Why wasn't he starting to heal already?* Most shifters healed faster than humans. This situation confused me.

"Hey, how are you feeling?" I asked.

"I'll survive." He took a swig from the water bottle in his hand.

"Good." I couldn't seem to find anything else to say, so I kept my mouth shut.

"Would you like me to drop you off at your truck?" Tristan asked.

"That'd be perfect. Thank you." Conrad looked down at his shirt, as if he were assuring himself it was properly buttoned up.

"I could take you, if you want." I didn't understand why I felt so guilty. I wasn't totally to blame. Besides, we might never have learned about his dragon gene had he not wandered into the cave.

"I'll go with Tristan, but thank you." His tone was hard, and I could tell he was upset with me. I probably deserved it . . . a little. But

I refused to waste too much time feeling remorse. We were both at fault.

Tristan followed Conrad out the door. Before closing it behind him, he turned to me and smiled. "It'll all work out fine. You'll see."

I hoped he was right. My life always seemed to be unnecessarily complicated.

CHAPTER 12

CONRAD

*S*ilence hung in the air during the trip from Tristan's home to the spot where I'd parked my truck. I'd refused to see a doctor, and Tristan had expressed his concern over that. He was a nice guy and genuinely cared about people. It's one of the reasons he was so easy to like. I couldn't say I'd ever clicked with a friend as quickly as I did with him, which was a nice change from my usual routine of isolation. I worked alone, and I lived alone. All my adult life, I'd only known a solitary existence. My earliest memories were of growing up in foster care, moving from one family to the next, but never settling anywhere. I'd always assumed that I was destined to be a rambler.

We pulled up behind my truck, and I dug my keys out of my pocket. "Thanks, Tristan. I appreciate the ride, the injury care . . ." I gestured to my head. "All of it."

"You're welcome." He smiled.

I opened the car door and climbed out of the seat.

"Hey, Conrad." Tristan leaned across the seat and looked up at me. "Don't be too upset with Jetta. She's been through a lot over the years. She may seem like a lunatic at times, but I promise she has her reasons for the things she does."

I nodded. "I'll keep that in mind."

I shut the door, and he waved as he pulled onto the roadway. I stood by my driver door until he was out of sight, then put my keys back in my pocket. I knew the box was in that cave, and I still had a job to do.

It only took me about twenty minutes to find the spot where the trail veered from the direction of the cave. The sun was starting to set, and the only flashlight I had was on my phone, so I needed to make this quick.

I retraced my previous steps and entered the cave with less trepidation than before. I turned on the flashlight app from my phone and immediately went to the room Jetta had been in before she'd knocked me out. My head still throbbed where she'd hit me, but the ibuprofen I'd taken was helping.

After stepping into the larger room, I took a moment to appreciate the sheer magnitude of the cavern. The space was enormous, and you'd never know from the outside that something so massive lay behind the small waterfall.

As I moved the light around the room, it glinted off a wall on the opposite side, and I moved closer to inspect it. The sides of the cavern were embedded with a smattering of rocks. There appeared to be crystals of some sort, but I had no idea what they were. That wasn't my area of expertise.

I shined my light toward the floor, looking for any signs of the box. Nothing. I supposed she could have taken it back to her car while I was out cold, but I doubted it. I didn't remember seeing it as she drove me back to town. My gut told me she'd left it in the cave.

She'd said she hit me with a shovel, so there was a good possibility she'd been digging. I started searching for areas in the dirt that had been freshly excavated. Sure enough, there was a spot toward the back of the room that had been dug up and repacked.

I located the offending shovel and put it to work. In minutes, I had the lockbox in my possession.

"You've caused a lot of trouble," I said as I inspected the metal box. The digital keypad and display were covered in dirt from where she'd buried it so haphazardly. It puzzled me that she hadn't put it in something to protect it. Unprotected electronics encased in the earth would eventually ruin the circuits.

I wiped it clean with my sleeve and looked it over one last time before repacking the dirt and putting the shovel back where I'd found it. With any luck, she'd never know I took it. At least, not until I was long gone, and this fiasco was behind me.

The thought of leaving Havenwood Falls was a tad bittersweet. I had things to attend to back in Atlanta, before I could move on with my life, but the little canyon was starting to grow on me in the short time I'd been there.

I tucked the box under my jacket and left the cave. Time to call Brandt and make a deal.

CELL SERVICE once again proved to be a challenge. I'd decided to just send him a text message, knowing it'd go through when my phone eventually caught a signal. I was ready for a hot shower and a warm bed. My mind flashed to Jetta. A certain willing woman would have been welcome as well, but the reality was that no matter how much I wanted her, avoiding that complication was for the best. I'd already made things difficult by becoming too invested in her. It's why I wanted to amend the deal we'd made to bring her back. She was happy here. Brandt would have his box back. All's well that ends well. I'd be fine taking less payment if it meant he'd leave her alone.

I stashed the box inside my duffel bag and shuffled to the bathroom to start the shower. I let it run while I brushed my teeth, then stepped beneath the hot water and sighed. The feeling was heaven on my sore muscles.

Once I'd washed, the exhaustion from the day hit me hard. I couldn't wait to fall into that bed. I wrapped the towel low around my hips and left the bathroom.

"Well, that's a new look. I hadn't pegged you as a skirt kinda man." Jetta's voice startled me.

"Holy shit," I barked. "How'd you get in here?" I quickly shifted my glance to my duffel bag, assuring it had been undisturbed.

"The door was unlocked." She reclined on the bed, her legs crossed in front of her. "I did knock. When you didn't answer, I got worried."

I gave her a knowing smirk. "You were worried about me? That's sweet."

Jetta released a sigh. "Don't make it weird. You could have a concussion. I just wanted to check on you."

"Uh huh," I said, letting her know I didn't believe that was the only reason she was there. "So, you being here, on my bed, while I'm in nothing but a towel. That's you checking on my wellbeing and has absolutely nothing to do with you wanting me."

She frowned. "Why do you have such a dirty mind?" she grumbled.

I stepped closer to her. "Why do you constantly elicit dirty thoughts?"

"So, you're blaming me for your perversions now?" She scooted off the bed and stood in front of me.

"I'm blaming your dream-catcher tattoo."

She grinned. "It is pretty spectacular."

I stepped closer, no longer caring why I shouldn't touch her. "So are you."

Jetta said nothing, but I could feel her shiver from where I stood. Every time I tried to deny that there was something unusual between us, something else would happen that proved me wrong. I could feel her around me. She gave off an energy that drew me in like a magnet. The more time I spent with her, the stronger it grew. I was now at a place where I could no longer resist. I wanted her. Needed her. To hell with Brandt and his money. To hell with my promise to avoid complications. This woman was complicated as hell, and I wanted to be lost in that forever.

"Jetta," I whispered, and her eyes locked with mine. "I want you."

Her lips parted, and she inhaled a deep breath. "I want you, too."

I pulled her to me and kissed her, funneling all my pent-up need into that one action. Breaking my lips from hers, I trailed kisses down her neck. My blood heated as I ran my hands over her body, savoring each curve. She put her arms around my neck and pulled at my hair. I picked her up and carried her to the bed, carefully laying her down before covering her body with mine.

Her lips explored my collarbone as I blindly worked the buttons on her shirt. I pulled back, so I could see what I was doing, and she closed her eyes, tilting her head back. She was so damn beautiful. She was everything I never knew I wanted in a woman. Smart, independent, sexy. And I was about to make her mine.

My body screamed for me to hurry up, but my mind suggested I be sure she understood the ramifications of what we were about to do. This was more than just sex. The feeling that she was made just for me became an incessant pounding in my head. *Mine. Mine. Mine.*

I realized then that if we took this step, I could never walk away. And I needed to be sure we were on the same page.

"Jetta," I whispered near her ear as I kissed up her jawline. "We should talk."

"No," she moaned. "We can talk after." I felt her hand slide between us, her fingers pulling at my towel that had somehow managed to stay on during our tumble to the bed.

"Baby, I'm serious. Before this goes any further, we need to talk expectations." I kissed her lips just as she found my hard length and squeezed. Anything I'd wanted to say fled my brain.

"Conrad." She raised her head up and lightly bit my earlobe. "Shut up and make me scream your name."

Loud banging on the door broke us out of our desire-fueled frenzy.

"What the hell?" I muttered. "Go away!"

The banging started again, but this time even more insistent.

"This had better be important," I said, "or someone is dead."

I grabbed my jeans and slipped them on, glancing at Jetta as she quickly buttoned her shirt. When I opened the door, a creepy elderly man with a cane stood on the other side.

"Can I help you?" I said in an annoyed tone. I mean, he did just interrupt what was sure to be some of the hottest foreplay I'd ever had.

"Where is my daughter?" The old man's voice came across as an animalistic growl, and for a moment, I was taken aback.

"Oh, hell no." Jetta's voice was full of fury as she leapt off the bed and joined me at the door. "What do you want?"

"What I want," said the old man, "is for you to stop destroying the family name." He stepped across the threshold and then around us as he moved to sit in the only chair in the room.

Jetta put her hands on her hips. "Conrad, this is my father, Lawrence Mills."

I nodded. "Nice to meet you, sir."

His green eyes met mine, and his bushy eyebrows rose above them as if to say, "Is it really?"

He turned his gaze back to his daughter. "You've been back less than a week and are already in a mess of trouble."

Jetta paled. "I don't know what you're talking about."

He leveled a hard stare at her. "You were seen yesterday morning with Bradly Russo."

She pushed out a breath that resembled relief. "It was nothing. He asked for my help. I said no. We went our separate ways."

"He's dead, Jetta. Rusty Higgins found Bradly's body while patrolling the woods. He'd been torn to shreds."

She gasped. "That's horrible."

Lawrence's expression was grim. "You were the last person seen with him. And you were asking about him last night. He's now dead. And Sheriff Kasun found an unusual ring among his belongings." His eyes narrowed at her. "You wouldn't know anything about a warded ring, would you?"

She put her hands on her hips. "Not a damn thing. Now, you listen to me, you old codger. I did not kill Bradly. He'd told me he was leaving town in a hurry. My guess is he crossed the wrong person one too many times and it finally caught up with him." She pointed a finger at him. "As for the Court, you tell them I don't know shit about any ring and they are barking up the wrong tree."

I watched this odd exchange with interest. Warded ring? The Court? Damn, the people in this town were strange.

"When did he die?" I asked.

Lawrence turned his irritated gaze on me. "They believe late last night."

I nodded. "It couldn't have possibly been Jetta. We were having dinner at Tristan's, then spent the rest of the evening together."

Jetta's eyes quickly shifted to mine in surprise, and I thought I saw a glint of gratitude.

"And I'm supposed to take your word for it?"

The old man had a point. I was a stranger in town, so I wasn't exactly a solid character witness.

"Daddy, do you really think so little of me that you believe I'd kill someone?" Her question obviously held more than what was visible on the surface. There was a hint of pain in her voice.

"Of course not," he snapped. "But that ring is another matter altogether."

She shook her head. "Again, I have no idea what you're talking about."

Lawrence stood and looked me up and down, then spoke to Jetta. "Don't get pregnant. You'd make a lousy mother."

Her mouth went slack, and my muscles became rigid as my fists balled at my sides. What kind of asshole father says something so cold to his daughter?

I felt Jetta's hand on my back. "Let it go. It's not worth the trouble."

Lawrence walked out the door without so much as a goodbye.

CHAPTER 13

JETTA

I should have been used to my father's insults by now, but his words still stung. Conrad's demeanor proved he had never witnessed such contempt for one's offspring before, although in truth, I wasn't biologically Lawrence's daughter.

"Are you okay?" Conrad rubbed his hands up and down my arms in a soothing manner.

"Yeah, I'm used to it." I moved to sit on the bed.

Conrad followed. "So, what's his problem?"

I shrugged. "Me."

"Seriously?"

I nodded. "More or less."

"What a dick." Conrad spat out the words in anger. I was moved that he felt the need to defend me.

I sighed. "My dad and I haven't gotten along in years. He doesn't like my hair, my music, my tattoos. He really hates my piercings." I laughed. "He says I look like a pin cushion." I ran a hand over my face. "But I think it really stems from the fact that I'm adopted. I'm not his actual flesh and blood, so despite taking me in, he doesn't feel I can accurately represent the family."

Conrad frowned as he sat next to me. "That's not fair. It's not your fault."

"No," I said. "It's not. But when I was a teen, I decided I wanted to know who my biological parents were, and he went ballistic. He felt I was ungrateful to be in the prestigious Mills family. My search took me nowhere, but in the process, I spent some time discovering who I really was inside. It led to my pursuit of music and my individuality. Dad really hated that. He feels a woman should be ruled by her father, and then later by her husband. I refused to live under his thumb or by his rules. We've been at odds ever since. I've kinda made it my life's goal to remind him at every turn that he doesn't own me or run my life."

Conrad smiled. "And he hates that."

"So much." I laughed.

"I don't know my parents either." Conrad absentmindedly rubbed his wrist. The same spot where his cuff usually was.

My interest was piqued. Maybe he'd tell me something that would lead to understanding his background and why he'd forgotten it.

"Really? Tell me about it." I leaned against his shoulder, hoping the intimacy would help him relax.

Conrad put an arm around me. "Not much to tell really. I bounced around from foster home to foster home for as long as I could remember. I never seemed to find the right fit. Once I was old enough to be on my own, I started traveling around the country, doing odd jobs."

I reached for his hand and laced my fingers through his. That's when I saw it. The tattoo on the inside of his right wrist.

"Conrad. Your tattoo matches the ring at my brother's shop." The surprise was evident in my voice.

He pulled his hand back. "Yeah. It's weird."

I reached for his hand once more and placed it in my lap, palm up. I traced the lines of the triskele with my fingertips. "When did you get this?"

He shook his head. "I don't remember."

I frowned. "None of this makes sense."

He let out a self-deprecating laugh. "Well, I have made some stupid decisions while I was drunk."

"No," I said. "I mean the ring. The tattoo. Your lack of memories."

He frowned. "Yeah, the ring and tattoo are weird, but I'm not missing memories. My life just hasn't been that memorable."

I shook my head. "There's more to all this. I just haven't figured it out yet."

He turned my face to his. "It's not important."

He kissed me gently, and I felt the tension from the confrontation with my father melt away.

"Listen, about earlier." I ran my fingers over his beard. "I'd love to pick up where we left off, but after hearing about Bradly, I think I'd better go. I need to be sure they aren't trying to pin this on me."

He nodded. "I understand."

"I promise I'll be back." I kissed him again.

"It's late anyway. I should get some sleep. We have tomorrow, right?" he asked.

"We do," I said. "And the next day, and the day after that."

I WENT to my room and made a few phone calls to be sure the Bradly thing had been properly dealt with. All was clear there, as everyone else had come to the same conclusion I did—his past had finally caught up with him. I went to bed knowing that wasn't going to chase me around the rest of my life. The only thing that kept me from a truly good night of rest was this dragon situation with Conrad. There was a connection with his tattoo and the ring. There had to be. If there was anything I'd learned over the years, it's that you needed ties to your past. To align the origins of your existence with who you are now. Somehow, that symbol meant answers for Conrad.

The following morning, I walked into my brother's pawn shop with one purpose in mind. The ring.

"Tristan, I think that ring belongs to Conrad." I crouched down and studied it through the glass case.

"I think it does, too." He was scribbling something on a notepad.

"We need to give it to him," I said.

"I'm fine with that." Tristan crossed his arms. "What are you thinking?"

"I don't know. It's just this gut feeling that he's supposed to be wearing that ring. It's like a family heirloom or something."

I couldn't shake the thought that this was why he was meant to come to Havenwood Falls. This explained why he was able to stumble across our little town.

"Since when did you become so sentimental?" Tristan teased.

I shrugged. "It's not sentiment. It's magic. Or fate. I don't know. You've always told me what's meant to be will be, right?"

He nodded. "I still believe that."

"This ring might just convince me that you're correct."

Tristan handed me the ring, and I examined it closely. The smooth metal was cold to the touch. The embossing was flawless.

"You should be the one to give it to him." Tristan handed me a ring box to keep it in.

Butterflies danced in my stomach at the thought of what his could mean for Conrad. What would happen when he finally put the ring on? Nothing? Everything? A part of me would be terribly disappointed if I were wrong. Maybe I was a *little* sentimental.

"Thanks." I placed the ring in the box and closed the lid.

"Be careful, Jetta. If that is the key to restoring his memories, there is no telling how he'll react."

"Good point. I don't know how it will affect him, but I do know this —Conrad would never hurt me." His integrity and protective nature were two things about Conrad I felt sure of.

CHAPTER 14

CONRAD

I woke up to the buzzing of my phone. The pain in my head had thankfully diminished to a dull ache. I rolled over and looked at the caller ID.

"Hello," I said, my voice still gruff from sleep.

"Well, you're still alive." Brandt's snarky tone came through loud and clear.

"I am. If you don't lose the snark, I won't be able to say the same for you." I was tired. Sore. And had no patience for his asshole behavior.

"Do you always threaten your employers?" He'd gone from sarcastic to pissed.

"Only the ones that treat me like shit." I sat up.

"I've treated you rather well, Conrad, and yet at every turn, you blow me off. I want an update, and it had better be good."

"Fine," I said. "I retrieved your box last night."

"Excellent. It's about time." I could almost hear his conniving grin. "And Jetta?"

"That's a little more complicated," I said. "I have your belongings. It might just be best to let her go."

"No." Brandt's resolve was firm.

"She's not gonna come willingly." I needed to make him see reason.

"Then force her."

"I can't kidnap her." I couldn't believe he was suggesting such a thing.

"Okay, then blackmail her. Remind her that we have the box, and if she knows what's good for her, she'll come back to me quietly."

"What's good for her?" I asked. "What does that mean?" Anger rose in my chest at the very thought of him threatening her.

"That's none of your business. She'll know what it means, and that's all that matters." He hung up without another word.

From the moment I walked into Brandt's office, I'd known he was slime, but there was a lot more to this story than he was telling me. I had to find out what information he'd omitted from his account of that night.

Just as I'd pulled on my jeans, a knock sounded at my door. Shirtless and barefoot, I opened the door to find Jetta on the other side.

I admired the view. "Well, you are a sight for sore eyes."

"Am I?" She looked at my bare chest. "I'd have to say the same about you."

I chuckled and opened the door wider. "Please, come in."

"Actually, I'd like to take you somewhere." She was tapping her fingers on her thighs nervously.

"Okay. Give me a minute to finish getting dressed." I left the door open and grabbed a shirt from the closet. Jetta stood in the doorway and watched me, her eyes following every movement I made. I could feel her gaze even when my back was turned. All she did was stand there, and she was turning me on.

"Okay." I motioned. "After you."

I shut the door behind me and followed her down the steps and out to her Jeep. Once inside, we drove out of town, and I realized she was taking the same road we'd been on the day before.

"Where are we going?" My curiosity was piqued.

"I'm taking you back to my cave." She quickly glanced at me, I assumed to gauge my reaction.

"Okay. Why?" I reached up and felt the slightly smaller knot on my forehead. "It's not like I have good memories there."

She pursed her lips together, and for a moment, I thought she wasn't going to answer. "I hope to change that today. I want to give you good memories."

"Well . . ." I shifted in my seat, so I could face her more. "I like where this is going." I envisioned a blanket on the ground, the waterfall behind us, and Jetta naked underneath me.

"Umm, probably not the direction you're thinking." Her expression was serious.

"Damn. Can we change that? Because the map I was following was pretty hot."

She chuckled. "Maybe afterward."

"After what?" I asked. Now I was really curious.

"You'll see." She gave me a wink.

Before long, we'd reached the trail she'd used to climb to the falls. We walked in silence. Several times I'd wanted to say something, but each time I opened my mouth, I found myself at a loss for conversation. Sometimes silence was a good thing.

We reached the falls, and she led me to the mouth of the cave. "Do you remember my telling you that only special people could enter the cave?"

I nodded, also remembering that I'd entered it again last night and that I now had her box. It dawned on me then that she might be bringing me there to show me the contents of the box. My throat constricted, knowing she'd freak when she learned her hiding place had been discovered.

"I know you thought I was crazy, but I want to show you what I was talking about." She took my hand and led me through the curtain of darkness into the first large room.

My eyes darted around, silently praying she didn't want to enter the larger room, where she'd buried the box.

She lit the wall sconces, and the cave became considerably brighter. We stood in the middle of the room, and Jetta held up my right hand. Her fingers trailed over the leather cuff.

"May I?" she asked.

I nodded, unsure what the purpose of removing it was.

She unsnapped it and put it in the pocket of her jacket, then she pulled out a ring box.

"Are you proposing to me?" I teased. "Because if so, let me warn you. I'm old-fashioned. I'm all about empowering women, but when it comes to marriage, a man still likes to do things the traditional way now and then."

She rolled her eyes. "Not even close, lover boy."

She opened the ring box and held it out to me. Inside was the ring that matched my tattoo.

I took a step back. "What is this?"

"It's yours, Conrad. Tristan and I firmly believe this is supposed to belong to you." She pushed the ring toward me.

"No." I couldn't. Something about that ring didn't sit right with me. I'd felt sure I'd regret having anything to do with it.

"Conrad," she said softly. "Please, just trust me on this. This ring will be life-changing."

"That's what I'm afraid of," I muttered.

"You're afraid?" She ran a hand down my chest. "My big, bad biker hunk is afraid?"

I swallowed hard. "Yes," I admitted. "And how did you know I'm a biker?"

"It's written all over you." She still had her hand on my chest. I loved feeling her touch me. It calmed and excited me all at once.

"So, I'm a hunk? And I'm yours?" I couldn't resist pointing out her change of heart. Obviously, she'd changed her mind sometime last night while in my room, but this was the first time she'd verbally admitted we might be something more than friends.

"Maybe," she teased. "But before we can explore that, you need to conquer this." She pulled the ring from the box. "Please, Conrad. Trust me."

I stared at the ring for a minute more before nodding my head. She took my right hand and looked into my eyes.

"No matter what happens, remember I am right here beside you. I won't leave."

That sounded ominous. "Okay."

She inspected the ring and then my fingers. She must have determined that the ring would fit best on my ring finger because that's the one she chose and slid it over my knuckles. Then she clasped my hand closed and stepped back.

My hand burned where the ring touched my skin. It traveled to my other fingers, then my palm, then to my wrist. I watched in shock as an odd orange glow followed the fiery path of my black tattoo, as if bringing it to life. The burning I felt on occasion became more like an inferno.

I closed my eyes, and images began to flash through my mind. My mother, her soft brown eyes and round face, appeared before me.

She kissed my forehead and sighed. "I hate to do this, son. But I've been left no choice. I'm dying, and the world can't ever know about you. The only way to protect you is if you forget who you are."

I felt tears run down my cheeks, but I was too lost in the memories to bother wiping them away.

My mother took me to a strange woman's house. The woman said some weird words I didn't understand, and I fell into a trance of sorts. The woman then tattooed my wrist with the triskele.

She handed my mother a small box. "If your situation ever changes, this ring will bring it all back. But for now . . ." She looked at me. "By tomorrow he'll remember nothing of his past. He will be unable to shift into his dragon form. When he comes of age, that tattoo will become visible and will allow him to seek the truth, should he desire it."

My mother hugged me and sobbed. "My sweet Conrad. Please forgive me. I have to let you go so that I may save you."

I sucked in a deep breath. Images of fire and molten rock ran through my mind. The ruins I'd been so obsessed with as a child had been a castle once, a part of our family heritage for centuries, before time and humanity had destroyed it all.

The most terrifying vision of all hit me with such force that it brought me to my knees. My dragon. The beast was fierce and angry. Two long twisted horns jutted from its enormous head. Black scales covered every inch of its body, except the leathery red wings that extended from the shoulder blades and the crest of fire that ran from the top of its head down to the bottom of its neck. The beard matched the crest, tendrils dripping like magma from its chin. Eyes the size of tractor tires stared back at me, the slanted pupils restricting and contracting as if trying to focus. The yellow irises glowed like embers.

I closed my mind to the horrendous beast, not wanting to believe what I was seeing. Then I was racked with a pain unlike anything I'd ever experienced. Bones cracked. Muscles stretched. Skin tore. When I opened my eyes again, I was standing in the cave, my head almost brushing the top of the cavern ceiling. Jetta stood before me, a small human figure with a large smile on her face. *Holy shit! How is this possible? And why isn't Jetta running for her life?*

I bent my head, and she walked toward me. I let out an involuntary snort, and flames shot from my nostrils.

Jetta jumped back. "Whoa, big fella. We're gonna have to get that under control. We can't have you roasting the villagers. Or me."

She stepped closer again, approaching from the right side of my face. Her hand reached out to stroke my scales, and despite our obvious differences, I still felt that spark of desire she'd always sent through me.

My mind reeled. How did I forget I was a lava dragon? Obviously, my mother was hiding me in plain sight, but how was it possible to lose the memories of something so significant? This was a lot to take in, and I knew I'd need time to adjust to finding myself after almost two decades of being lost.

Jetta brought my attention back to her. "Conrad, I'm a frost dragon. This cave is warded so that only dragons can enter."

Jetta's a dragon, too? I felt sure I was losing my mind. A range of emotions rushed through me: loss, anger, confusion, relief. I hated the events that led me to this place in my life, yet I was happy to find my way back to the truth. Elated that I was no longer alone in a world in which I'd felt I'd never belonged.

She quickly removed her clothes. The human side of me was thrilled for the show, but I had no idea what she was doing.

She stepped back and closed her eyes. I watched in fascination as she transformed before me. Beautiful white scales replaced milky porcelain skin. Her silver hair morphed into a crown of horns that surrounded her head and neck. She was only a few feet shorter than I was once she'd fully shifted. She was gorgeous as a human, and gorgeous as a dragon. Her eyes were the same icy blue as in her human form, and I couldn't help but stare into them as I allowed the implication of this transformation to wash over me.

We were both dragons. On opposite ends of the spectrum, but dragons just the same. Our dragon genes recognized each other, long before we did. We were drawn to each other so desperately because we were meant to be each other's mates. She was mine, and I was hers. Now that I'd found where I belonged, and who I belonged to, I was never letting go.

CHAPTER 15

JETTA

*H*e was beautiful. I'd never met a lava dragon, but I'd read about them. Conrad was damn amazing. Simon, on the other hand, was a fire dragon. The distinction was small, but a distinction nonetheless. Lava dragons appeared to be made of the very molten rock they were named after, where fire dragons were more like those you usually read about in fairy tales.

After a few moments of silence and a quick nuzzle of his neck, Conrad used his telepathic communication.

"I need to change back. This is too much, too fast."

"Absolutely," I said. "Just envision your human self, and it'll happen."

He looked down and noticed his clothes were shredded. "Ah, so now that makes sense."

I nodded.

"I might have a problem. I don't have clothes."

I thought about it a moment. "I think I have the solution."

We shifted to humans and ran back to the Jeep as quickly as possible.

Lucky for him, I always carried a change of clothes with me. They were pink sweat pants and a t-shirt, and they looked totally ridiculous on him, but he was thankful to have anything to cover his adorably naked ass. The sweats were snug on his hips, the elastic ankles only reaching mid-calf. He slipped the V-neck tee over his head and worked it down his torso. His muscles stretched the fabric to the point that when he bent over, it ripped up the side.

"Fuck it." He ripped it the rest of the way off and tossed it in the back seat.

"That was pretty hot," I said as I drove us back into town.

He grinned. "You think that's sexy? Wait until we get back to the room, and I rip off these sweats." He turned his eyes to me. "And then it's your turn."

I grinned. "I'm looking forward to that."

"So, tell me about the cave."

"It's been warded so only dragons can enter. My father purchased the cave before the settlement became a town. He knew we'd need someplace we could shift and be ourselves."

Conrad scratched his beard. "Settlement? How old is your dad?"

I smiled. "He's pushing two hundred."

Conrad choked. "He looks pretty good for his age." He paused. "Wait, how old are you?"

"It's rude to ask a woman her age. Lucky for you I don't care. I'm one hundred and two, but everyone thinks I'm twenty-eight."

He coughed. "Well then . . . let's change the subject."

I laughed. "Not into older women?"

He grinned. "Not usually, but I'm totally into you."

"What about you? How old?" It dawned on me he might not be the younger of the two of us.

"My memories are still a little fuzzy, but I believe I'm the age I look, so thirty." He frowned. "I'm gonna have to do some research to be sure."

He looked a little distressed over that lack of knowledge, so I obliged his earlier request and changed the subject. "Did you know our cave has diamonds?"

He shook his head. "Really?"

"Yep, it's where we get some of the family fortune. I'd wager it was another reason my greedy father bought it up before someone else had a chance. He doesn't do anything half-assed. He researches the hell out of every deal he makes." As an aside I threw in, "We don't own the falls, just the cave."

"So, you're loaded and beautiful. I'm a lucky guy." He winked and skimmed his fingers along the back of my neck, sending shivers down my spine.

"You are. And I haven't even had a chance to show you my talents in bed."

He closed his eyes and groaned. "You're killing me, woman."

We pulled up in front of the inn, and I glanced up at the window of my room. "How quickly do you think we can get up there?"

He shrugged. "Not quick enough. I don't want to wait another minute."

We walked into the inn, hand in hand. Conrad was on the receiving end of some odd stares, but we didn't care. We were too lost in each other.

I was amazed at how my life had changed in just a few short days. Weeks ago I was fighting to escape the worst relationship of my life. Now here I stood, next to the man I felt sure was my soul mate. I'd never considered myself the kind of girl who would settle down. But the truth hit me square in the face. The right person can change everything. Not that I was gonna turn into Betty Crocker anytime soon, but for once, I could envision a lifetime spent with someone by my side. Someone who would love, protect, and comfort me. Someone who wouldn't try to change me or fit me into a mold of his choosing. He wanted me just as I was. He was perfect as he was, too. And he was mine. There was no doubt. We'd connected on a level that only dragons could understand. We'd become linked in a way that was deep, meaningful, and beyond the limits of the natural world.

Now that his dragon had emerged, he'd have to register with the Court, but that should be an easy task.

I was truly happy, even with all the other shit life threw at me. I had someone who would stand by my side as I jumped those hurdles that before I'd always had to face alone.

My room was closest to the stairs, but Conrad needed clothes that fit him. I pushed him forward as we treaded the short hallway that led to his door. Conrad swung it open. My blood froze in my veins, and my stomach soured. Brandt Sawyer sat on the overstuffed chair in Conrad's room. The lockbox I'd buried on his lap.

"Hello, sweetheart. I've missed you." Brandt's smile was wide, but the sentiment didn't reach his eyes. He was furious with me.

"How in the hell?" I wanted to run, but my legs wouldn't cooperate. My feet were rooted in place.

I sensed Conrad tense up next to me. I'd have to explain why this strange man was here, sitting on his bed, using terms of endearment toward me. How did he find me? How did he know I'd be with Conrad?

Brandt held up the box, and I felt the bile rise in my throat. "Thanks for your help, Conrad. I couldn't have located this without you."

The words didn't register immediately, but my hand went slack in Conrad's grip.

"Why are you here?" Conrad demanded between clenched teeth.

Brandt stood. "Well, you know what they say. If you want something done right, you have to do it yourself." He handed the box to a large man standing to his left. I assumed the bodyguard-looking buffoon was one of his goons from the bar. "You were taking far too long, Conrad. I didn't pay you to play house."

His stare went straight to our clasped hands.

I stepped back. "Conrad? What is he talking about?"

I was going to be sick. I couldn't believe what I was hearing. I didn't *want* to believe it.

"Jetta, let me explain." Pain filled his expression.

"You son of a bitch." My hurt and anger bubbled to the surface. I couldn't believe I'd let my guard down again. I'd *trusted* him.

"Aw, how touching. You really must have had her going, Conrad. She doesn't usually become so emotional over the men she screws." Brandt's barb hit its mark. Conrad lunged at Brandt, but the oversized bodyguard beside him stopped him from reaching the smug-faced prick now standing by the bed. I could tell Conrad was fighting for control of his emotions. With his dragon and memories back, he needed a tight rein to avoid an incident.

Brandt motioned for me to come closer. "Let's explain to Conrad how important it is that you, and he, cooperate with me."

I stepped in the room and shut the door behind me. Brandt wasn't going to tell Conrad anything he didn't already know, but if he left town with the contents of that box . . . none of our kind would be safe.

"Have a seat, Conrad. I have a few things you should see." Brandt unlocked the box and pulled out a large manila envelope. Inside was a sandwich-sized zip-lock bag containing bloody white scales. I cringed as I remembered the events that led up to him cutting those scales off my tail. Conrad hadn't moved, so Brandt nodded to the larger man. "Chance, would you mind?"

Chance pushed Conrad to sit on the bed.

"Do you know what these are, Conrad?" Brandt shook the bag in front of Conrad's face. "No, of course you don't. How could you?" He pulled a cell phone from the box next. "I could tell you, but you'd never believe me. So how about I show you?"

Brandt moved to sit next to Conrad and lowered the phone into Conrad's field of vision. I didn't need to see the video he was about to display. I'd lived it.

"Brace yourself." Brandt tapped play. I saw the change in lighting flash across Conrad's face as the audio took me back to that night.

I'd gone to dinner with Brandt after a couple of weeks of him badgering me for a date. After dinner, we'd gone back to the club to discuss a new set. I'd wanted to change my act up a bit to keep it fresh for the regular patrons. Brandt wasn't interested in work. I'd grown angry and stormed out the back door. He'd chased me outside and pushed me against a wall. I pushed back but couldn't shove him off me. In a panic, I'd shifted. That's where the video began.

Conrad frowned as he watched the visual evidence of my dragon's existence. Brandt's voice was loud and clear over the phone's speaker.

"What the hell are you?" he shrieked as his shaky hands worked the camera.

My responding growl was clear and predatory.

"Well, whatever you are, Jetta Mills, I've now got proof." You could hear the click of Brandt's switchblade. He lunged for me and missed. I'd done my best to escape, praying no one had seen me yet and I could shift back to my human form. As I turned my back on Brandt, he swiped at my tail and removed a few scales in the process. Instinct kicked in, and I jerked my tail back and forth, causing Brandt to slice the skin on his own cheek.

I moved behind a neighboring building that was thankfully abandoned and shifted to my human self. My back was bloody where he'd taken the scales. Brandt had captured the whole thing on his phone.

Brandt stopped the video. "I'm sure now you can see why I not only wanted the lockbox back, but also Jetta." He shook his head, clearly enjoying his victory. "You had no idea you were being duped by a monster."

He put the phone back into the box and placed the scales on top of it. "Jetta, love, why don't you tell Conrad the rest."

I cleared my throat. "It's not hard to guess what a douchebag like you would do with that kind of evidence."

Conrad refused to look at me. Damn him. This was his fault. Fury renewed within me, and I decided he deserved to hear every excruciating detail. He needed to know who'd he'd aligned himself with. He needed to understand what his betrayal could cost me, and what it had just cost him.

I crossed my arms in front of me. "Brandt found me hiding behind a bush, bare-ass naked and bleeding. He had my scales in a handkerchief and the cell phone in his hand. I knew he had me. He forced me back into the club through the rear door, then allowed me to grab a change of clothes from the small area I called my dressing room." I took a deep breath. "We were both bleeding."

I fought back my own rage as I recalled his actions. "He downloaded the additional video from the security feed to his phone, which shows the entire indent, including my shifting from human to dragon. He then locked the evidence up in that box and put it in the safe. Then he told me I would not only continue to be his main act, but that he owned me, body and soul, or he'd show the world what I really was. I argued with him, and he called the police, claiming I'd broken into his safe and attacked him."

Brandt shrugged. "I thought a few hours in lockup would cool your jets. I knew they wouldn't believe a word you'd said. Hell, half the cops in that jurisdiction are on my payroll." He chuckled. "I could have kept you in there indefinitely, had I chosen to do so. You needed to see the kind of power I can wield, Jetta. I'm a king."

I glared at him.

"And then you decided to break into my safe for real and go on the run." He nodded at Conrad. "That's where you stepped in, Mr. Monroe." Brandt looked at me. "He's been keeping me apprised of his progress, for the most part. Then after a text from him wanting to renegotiate, I'd realized he'd fallen for you and wasn't going to cooperate with the rest of the plan. Finding this shithole town was a pain in the ass. We did some digging into the subject of dragons and found an individual with his own connections here. He lives right here in Havenwood Falls and travels out of town regularly for . . . business. He was willing to sell us the information we needed to find you both. We flew into Grand Junction, then met our new friend at a rest stop. With the right monetary motivation, he happily led us right into town. You can't outsmart me, sweetheart." His lecherous smile was vile and made me want to puke.

I knew the kind of person Brandt was describing. We had an underground element, such as Bradly, that would sell out their own grandmother if it brought them a profit. A handful who snuck in and out of town on short trips to do business, keeping their activities hidden as much as possible. Some dirt bag accepting money for a guide into town didn't surprise me much, but if caught, they'd face banishment—or worse. I did find it remarkable that Brandt was successful. A stranger in town, who wasn't welcomed by the town itself, was a rarity.

Once again, Brandt proved to be the lowest form of life in existence. Still, Conrad's deceit was more painful than anything Brandt had done to me. Brandt had cut my skin and tried to steal my dignity, but Conrad had shattered my heart.

CHAPTER 16

CONRAD

I was seriously pissed. Not only had Brandt played me, but he'd assaulted Jetta. And now he might have ruined my relationship with the only woman I'd likely ever love. My mate. My new reason to exist.

I couldn't bring myself to look at her. I deserved her hatred and scorn. Yes, I'd been fooled, but I should have followed my gut. I should have told her everything. Especially after I'd realized that Jetta wasn't the hardened criminal he'd made her out to be. But the truth was, I didn't care what she was, because I loved her and would have excused anything in her past.

"Jetta, I think he has us by the short and curlies," I said, giving her a look I hoped she'd recognize as a signal to play along.

"Don't talk to me," she growled.

"We need to tell him everything." *We need to get them out of town. Come on, Jetta. Get with the program.*

Brandt's eyes narrowed. "What are you leaving out, Jetta?"

She shook her head.

"She has a shitload of diamonds."

Jetta stared daggers at me. "Shut up, Benedict Arnold."

"Brandt, if we give you the diamonds, will you let Jetta go?" I prayed he'd take the bait.

"I'll consider it." I knew he was lying, but I'd take whatever we could get.

She continued to glare at me. "Fine. Whatever."

Brandt walked over to her and put his arm around her. He kissed her temple, and I wanted to rip his lips and hands off for even daring to touch her.

"Good girl," Brandt murmured in her ear. "Now, Conrad, you need to get dressed. You look like an idiot."

I grabbed a change of clothes and dressed quickly, not caring that there were three other people in the room.

Chance picked up the box and waited for me to finish putting on my shoes. I followed Jetta and Brandt out the door, with Chance taking up the rear. I knew how this would play out in Brandt's mind. We'd show him the diamonds, and Brandt would take what he could from the cave. Then he and Chance would leave with Jetta, the evidence, and the gems. My body would never be found again, and Brandt would take back what was left of the twenty-five thousand he'd already paid me.

We stepped outside, and Brandt led us to a black Humvee.

"Well, that's not obnoxious or conspicuous," I remarked.

Chance gave me a hard shove.

I turned and stared into his eyes. "If you value your hands, you'll keep them to yourself."

I sat in the front with the big fella, while Brandt sat in back with Jetta. I gave them directions to the trail, then we spent the rest of the drive listening to Brandt's incessant jabbering about how smart and powerful he was. Every now and then, I glanced back at Jetta and saw her staring out the window. She refused to acknowledge me. I hoped that someday I could make her understand that my intentions were pure, even if my results were less than desirable.

We reached the trail and resumed the same formation as before: Jetta next to Brandt, me in the middle, and Chance bringing up the rear.

Chance pulled out a gun and pointed it at my side. "If either of you try to run, Conrad dies."

I wasn't sure Jetta would care at that point, but I hoped she did. She nodded but didn't say a word. When we reached the waterfall, I addressed

Brandt. "The cave is behind the waterfall, but it's a little hard to reach. The entrance is that opening just to the right."

Brandt motioned to Chance. "Give me the gun and go check it out."

Chance handed over the weapon and cautiously made his way down the steps. I glanced at Jetta, but her expression gave nothing away. Brandt thought he had the upper hand, but he was about to learn that the only thing more dangerous than one dragon was two.

I took a step back and kicked off my shoes. Brandt's eyebrows drew together. "What the hell are you doing?"

I shrugged as I pulled my shirt over my head. "I know you plan to kill me." I unbuttoned my jeans.

Jetta's eyes flashed with understanding. She'd finally caught on to what I was doing. She pulled off her shirt as well, and Brandt's eyes went wide.

"What is wrong with you two? Are you hoping to freeze to death?"

Jetta stopped short of pulling down her jeans. "Do you want me to stop stripping?"

There was an alluring hint of wickedness to her voice, and I knew Brandt would be distracted by it.

He shook his head. "I will never complain about you getting naked in front of me."

"Then shut up." She continued taking off her clothes until she was in nothing but her underwear.

"Boss," yelled Chance. "There's nothing in here. Just a small, dark cave."

Brandt chuckled. "Nice distraction, but you've wasted your time."

"Not really," replied Jetta. "We got you out here, so I'd say we hit our objective."

She stepped back and began to shift. Brandt panicked and grabbed my arm, shoving the gun in my back.

"Now you listen to me, Jetta. Conrad dies if you don't change back." His voice was loud and authoritative, but fear laced his words.

Chance hurried up the steps, almost slipping a time or two. He reached our side and looked up at Jetta's dragon in awe.

"You overestimate her feelings for me." I shook my head. "She doesn't give a shit what you do to me."

Brandt responded by pushing the gun to my head. Jetta bent her head low, her focus on the gun. She snorted, and Chase jumped.

"Calm down, Brandt. I know how we can resolve this." I braced myself for impact.

Brandt's gaze turned on me, and that's when Jetta's tail came down hard behind us. It knocked us all off balance, but it gave me just enough space to jump away. I didn't waste a moment, shifting into a version of myself I'd long suppressed.

Brandt and Chase stepped away from me, their eyes widening in horror. While Jetta was beautiful, almost magical looking, I looked like something straight out of hell. I widened my stance and lowered my head, a rumble building in the back of my throat. When I opened my mouth, fire shot out like a flamethrower, and the two men threw themselves to the ground. They covered their heads in a futile attempt to protect themselves.

Brandt located some of his backbone and looked up at me, sheer terror still in his features. He held up his hands in a gesture of surrender as he cautiously stood.

"Let's talk about this." He tried to keep his tough guy persona, but he was visibly trembling, and his voice cracked as he spoke. Chase was frozen by fear, not moving an inch. Brandt kicked him, prodding him to move.

Jetta moved to stand beside me, and our telepathic communication took over. "We could drown them. The water in the falls is poisonous to humans."

"That might work," I said.

"But . . . I really don't want to get my hands dirty, so I have a better idea."

"I'm up for whatever you have planned." I shot another stream of fire above the men, just in case they had any ideas about running. "Jetta, I'm sorry about everything."

"Not now, Conrad. We'll talk later." She stood to her full height. "For now, follow my lead."

At that moment, Chase and Brandt made a beeline for the trees, almost stumbling as they leapt over small branches and rocks.

"Slight change of plans," Jetta said. "Catch them."

Jetta turned on her camouflage and instinct helped me follow suit. We took off in opposite directions, intending to cut them off before they ran very far.

Jetta lumbered alongside Chase as he ran. His terrified gaze darted around him. He could barely hear her, and he couldn't see her at all, but he had to know she was there. He pushed himself against a tree and looked as if he was trying to calm his breathing.

I was a few yards in the opposite direction. Once Chase was cornered, I gave my full attention to capturing Brandt as he ran directly in front of me. I focused on him and lowered my head, snorting out a stream of fire. Brandt screamed, then turned and shot at me. The first bullet missed by a mile, but the second grazed my cheek, leaving a trail of blood running down my jaw.

"Conrad!" screamed Jetta. She sounded terrified. I shot another stream of fire toward Brandt, and he hit the dirt, his hands attempting to protect his head as he curled into a fetal position.

"I'm okay. It's just a scratch," I said. "Get Chase."

She reached out her front claws and grabbed a screaming Chase. She tucked him in close to her body, effectively hiding them both in her camouflage. I did the same with Brandt, both men screaming like little girls at a horror movie.

I laughed as we rose into the air. Jetta was graceful, where my flying skills were in need of some practice.

"What's so funny?" she asked as we soared over the tops of trees and outcroppings.

"Listen to them. They sound like one of my foster moms when she saw a mouse."

Jetta laughed, too. "They really do." She paused and pointed one of her back claws toward the large falls not far from Fallview Tavern & Grille. "These two are gonna *love* the Alverson sisters."

"Who are they?" I asked.

"Sirens," Jetta replied.

"Damn, those exist?" I was in awe of this revelation.

"You have a lot to learn about Havenwood Falls." She paused. "All those monsters you were told about during your childhood? They're all real."

"Holy shit," I muttered.

"Exactly."

We slowed our descent and landed at the top of the falls. The men were silent now, and I wondered if they'd died of heart attacks during our short trip. Jetta placed her front paws on the ground and opened them slowly. Chase was white as a sheet, but still alive. He carefully stood up, then tried to run. He'd only made it a few steps when Jetta's large claw hooked the back of his shirt and pinned him to the ground.

I opened my paws as well but made sure not to let Brandt escape.

"What are we waiting for?" I asked.

"Simon," she said. "He can't hear us, but he knows we're here. He can sense it."

That was news to me.

Brandt mustered the courage to speak up. "Please, let us go. We'll never bother you again. Just let us go."

Jetta snorted in disbelief, frost escaping her nostrils as she made herself visible once more. I followed her lead, waiting to see what would happen next.

As she'd predicted, in less than five minutes a large, dark brown dragon landed behind us. Simon's voice boomed in my head. "What kind of trouble have you brought me now, woman?"

Astonishment banged around in my skull like a pinball machine. That explained why Simon thought he knew me. He was a dragon, too. I really needed a stiff drink.

"Looking good, Conrad. I knew you'd be an impressive specimen."

"Thanks. You're rather intimidating yourself."

Simon nodded his head in thanks. "Now, why are you here with two crying men under your paws?"

"A gift for the Alverson family."

Simon nodded. "They will be most appreciative." He paused. "No one will miss them?"

Jetta chuckled. "Not anyone that matters. In fact, you'll be doing the world a favor."

Simon nodded and stepped forward. We released Brandt and Chance as Simon scooped them both up into his grip. The men screamed loudly once again.

Before flying to the bottom of the falls, Simon chuckled. "These two should have never come to Havenwood Falls."

CHAPTER 17

CONRAD

I watched Simon land at the bottom of the falls and then disappear into some trees. Jetta camouflaged herself again, then walked to the edge of the falls and jumped, falling just a few feet before rising into the air like a giant kite. I followed her, trying to catch up. Using my wings still felt a bit awkward, not that I'd admit that to her.

"What will happen to them?" I asked.

"Do you really care? They were horrible humans. The world is better off without them." Her tone was flat.

"I agree. I'm just morbidly curious."

She slowed down a bit, and we glided side by side through the clouds. "The Alversons will keep them in a holding cell until the council has a chance to decide their fate. If I had a say, I'd let the sisters feed on them."

"Shit, that's gotta be a hell of way to go." It would take me a while to adjust to all this new information. Once my dragon returned, so did some of the stories my mother had told me. Most of them were dragon-related, but every now and then her stories had included a witch or a goblin. I'd always thought she was embellishing to make it interesting. I'll be damned if she wasn't telling the truth about all of it.

Jetta nodded. "In my opinion, men like Brandt need to be dealt with permanently. But that's not for me to decide. I'll testify against them, if the Court asks." She picked up speed again.

The view below us was stunning. Snow-covered caps jutted above waves of evergreens and pines. But nothing was more striking than Jetta flying over the peaks and valleys of the canyon. It wasn't just visual, although I could make out her outline easily despite her invisibility to the human eye. I could tell her spirit felt truly free up there. She was happy, for the most part.

We landed back at her cave, and she shifted back to her human form quickly. She jerked her clothing on in hasty motions as I shifted and moved to do the same.

I'd pulled my shoes on when she picked up the lockbox, removed the scales, and then hurled the rest into the pool of water at the base of the falls. Everything inside rained down in pieces before settling somewhere beneath the surface.

"Is it over? Will you be safe now?" I asked, truly worried she may have to face this again in the future.

"Yes, it's over." She held up the scales. "I'll keep these in the cave for now. Dragon scales are too valuable to leave lying around. They should be safe there, assuming some deceitful asshole dragon doesn't dig them back up and bring them out again."

"Jetta, you have every right to be angry with me. I should have told you the truth in the beginning. But I swear to you, I really believed you'd just taken random valuables from him. I didn't know the contents of the box until he showed them to me at the inn."

She hung her head, and her voice was soft. "I trusted you, Conrad."

"I know. As you said, I was a deceitful asshole. I'm sorry that I broke that trust." My heart ached, knowing I'd hurt her so deeply. "If it helps, once I'd gotten to know you, I'd decided I was only returning the box to Brandt, even if I had to forfeit the rest of my fee." I stepped toward her. "I'd realized shortly after I met you that regardless of what you'd taken, you weren't the criminal he said you were. I couldn't allow him to hurt you. If I'd only known the real story . . ." My voice trailed off in regret. "I'm so sorry, Jetta."

She shrugged. "Yes, you are a deceitful asshole, but if you'd known the real story, you never would have come to Havenwood Falls," she said. "I'd never have met you, and you may have never found yourself again."

I nodded. "True." I looked into her eyes. "But if it would have saved you all of this pain, I would do it all differently. I'd have stayed away forever if it would have protected you. I know it's hard to believe, after all I've done, but I love you. I think I have from the minute I saw you."

She took a moment to compose herself. "It's not how I would have preferred to have met you, but I believe you were supposed to be here. It's what was meant to be."

I looked at the tattoo on my wrist, the flames of it now a vivid red instead of the dull black it'd been before putting on the ring.

"Maybe you're right." I closed the distance between us until we were face to face. "No matter what happens from here on out, I owe you a debt of gratitude. You saved me. Before learning the truth, I was drifting from job to job, restless and unhappy. Never allowing myself any kind of meaningful relationships. Solitude was easier. I wanted to avoid the risk of being hurt. But now I feel I belong somewhere." I shook my head. "I wish Mama would have known about this place. We could have come here. She wouldn't have died alone or had to worry about who'd care for me later."

Jetta placed her hand on my cheek. "I wish she would have, too, but that ring got here somehow. We may never know the whole story, but someone expected you to find your way here one day and discover your truth. I'm glad I was able to help you with that." She kissed me gently.

My heart swelled at the love I still saw in her eyes. She didn't completely hate me.

As if she'd read my mind, she said, "Now, that doesn't mean I'm not gonna put you through hell to make you prove yourself. Payback is a bitch, Monroe. You have a lot of work ahead of you."

I nodded. "Yes, ma'am. I'll do my best."

Then I kissed her thoroughly.

WE SPENT the next couple of weeks making arrangements for me to stay in Havenwood Falls as a full-time resident. I went back to Atlanta and paid off my debts, thanks to a donation from Jetta's diamond collection and what was left of the money I'd gotten from Brandt. Then I hauled my motorcycle and what few belongings I owned back to Havenwood Falls. I rented a little house near the Havenstone development and began my search for a job. Jetta moved in with me.

I registered with the Court, and after hearing my story, they allowed Addie to make minor modifications to my current family tattoo. Besides infusing it with the town's magic, she also added something meaningful to me, per my request. I couldn't wait to show Jetta, so as soon as her set was done at Fallview Tavern & Grille, I rushed to carry her off the stage.

"What are you doing?" she hissed. "Put me down. Everyone is looking at us."

"Good," I said, "let them." I kissed her just to be sure there was plenty of fodder for the town gossips. I whispered in her ear, "I have something special to show you."

She chuckled. "Oh, I bet you do."

I shook my head. "And you say I'm the dirty-minded one."

She clutched at my neck as I hurried outside with her in my arms. I sat her down in front of my truck and rolled up my sleeve. I no longer wore the cuff.

She gasped. "Is that a snowflake?"

"Yes. I asked Addie to put it in the center of the triskele."

"But why?" Her beautiful eyes searched mine.

"For you, of course. You are the center of my universe. My happiness —my very life— revolves around your happiness." I bent down on one knee and took her hand. "Jetta Mills, will you make me the happiest deceitful asshole on earth and become my wife?"

She grinned at my use of her new nickname for me.

I kissed her fingers. "I don't have a ring yet, but I was hoping this could be our new family crest."

She traced the lines of the snowflake. "It's beautiful, Conrad." Her eyes met mine, and her usual mischievousness replaced the emotion I'd seen moments earlier. "You know, if I say no, you are totally screwed. You'll be stuck explaining that weird-ass tattoo for the rest of your life."

I shrugged. "It's a risk I was willing to take. I'll just tell people I was drunk."

She closed her eyes and pulled me to my feet. "Damn it."

"What?" I froze, wondering if she truly was going to say no. I felt my heart beat so hard I thought it would knock a hole in my chest.

"My dad is gonna be so happy that I'm marrying a dragon."

I picked her up and swung her around. "It'll be okay. We'll find other ways to make him miserable."

"We?" she asked.

"Oh yeah. We are in this together. I go where you go. I piss off who you piss off. It's a package deal."

Her smile turned devious as she took my hand in hers. "I can't wait to see what kind of trouble we'll get into."

WE HOPE you enjoyed this story in the Havenwood Falls series featuring a variety of supernatural creatures. The series is a collaborative effort by multiple authors.

Books in the main Havenwood Falls series:

Forget You Not by Kristie Cook
Old Wounds by Susan Burdorf
Fate, Love & Loyalty by E.J. Fechenda
Covetousness by Randi Cooley Wilson
The Winged & the Wicked by T.V. Hahn & Kristie Cook
Alpha's Queen by Lila Felix
Ink & Fire by R.K. Ryals
Lose You Not by Kristie Cook
Tragic Ink by Heather Hildenbrand
Nowhere to Hide by Belinda Boring
Flames Among the Frost by Amy Hale
Rock Me Gently by Susan Burdorf
From the Embers by Amy Miles (June 2018)
Defying Gravity by Kallie Ross (July 2018)

More books releasing on a monthly basis

Also try the YA line, Havenwood Falls High, and the historical paranormal line, Legends of Havenwood Falls

Stay up to date at www.HavenwoodFalls.com

Subscribe to our reader group and receive free stories and more!

ABOUT THE AUTHOR

Since childhood, bestselling and award-winning author Amy Hale has been creating exceptional stories that summon a whirlwind of emotions and inspiration unto the reader. She loves creating characters and worlds from nothing but her imagination and a few glasses of wine. Her love of the written word has not only resulted in her writing some of her readers' favorite adventures, but has also manifested itself in the form of book hoarding. She's convinced it's not a sickness.

She debuted her first fiction novel in 2015 after retiring from thirteen years of nonfiction writing for various online entities. For the last couple of decades, she's also carried the titles of Laundry Goddess, Chef, Butt Wiper, Soother of Temper Tantrums, and in more recent years, Moderator of Sarcastic Eyerolls and Sass. She resides in Illinois with her husband, as well as two grown children who claim they are never moving out. Regardless, they are the center of her universe, although her cat believes otherwise.

If she had any spare time, she'd love music, photography, watching Mystery Science Theater 3000 with her family, and long rides on the back of her husband's motorcycle.

Learn more at authoramyhale.com

ACKNOWLEDGMENTS

I always worry I will sound redundant while writing this page, but I firmly believe the words Thank You can never be said enough.

I give thanks to God and all he provides. My faith in Him has helped me through some pretty rough storms in recent years.

John, my husband, is the most amazing man I've ever known. He gives so much of himself and asks very little in return. He is the reason I keep trying. He's my support, my cheerleader, my shoulder to cry on. The things I've achieved so far are because he's given me the boost to climb higher. I love you more than words could ever say.

Thanks to Matt, Rachel, and Wes for understanding how crazy things get when I am on a deadline. You kids are the best.

Thanks to Kristie Cook for once again entrusting me with a small part of her amazing project that is Havenwood Falls. Jetta and Conrad were really fun to write and I'm looking forward to more of their story in the future.

Many thanks to Kristen Yard for allowing me the generous use of the Alverson sisters, Simon, and Fallview Tavern & Grille. I also want to thank Kristie Cook for allowing me to add Whisper Falls Inn, Madame Luiza Petran, and Sindi Scott to my story.

Thanks to Kristie Cook and Liz Ferry for your superb editing skills.

You ladies make my writing shine in ways I could never achieve on my own.

Thanks to Regina Wamba for once again creating the perfect cover. I'm ever in awe of your talent!

Thanks to my beta readers, Danielle, Ashley, Jenell, and Amber, for your input while I worked through this story.

Much love and gratitude to our growing Havenwood Falls family! I'm honored to work with some the most talented people I've ever met. You guys and gals keep me excited about this project and your support has meant the world to me.

To my readers, Thank You will never be enough. Your trust in my words, the use of my imagination, to entertain you is a feeling I can't describe. I hope I give back a fraction of the joy your readership gives me.

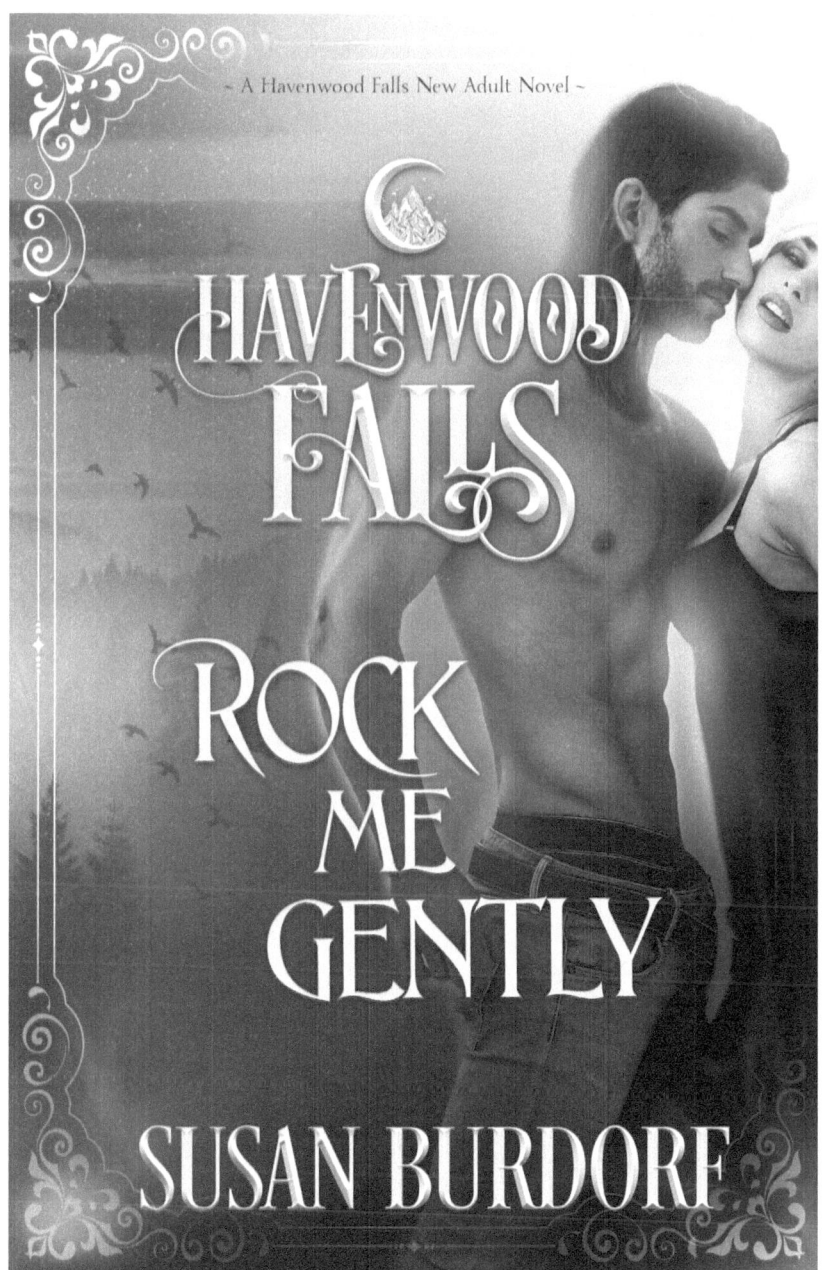

~ A Havenwood Falls New Adult Novel ~

HAVENWOOD FALLS

ROCK ME GENTLY

SUSAN BURDORF

AN EXCERPT

Rock Me Gently (A Havenwood Falls Novel) by Susan Burdorf

With his hard rock band Pink Melon nominated for a Grammy, lead singer Brett Rhys-Falwyck's dreams are about to come true. Then tragedy strikes. After losing the one person he loves most, he turns to the only thing he knows will never fail him—his music. But even that's betrayed by the corrupt owner of the band's management company that owns his soul. Turning his back on his bandmates, he finds himself in the mountains of Colorado—running a band camp, of all things.

Cecelia Amundson, angel and owner of Havenwood Falls Music & More, can't stop dreaming of a man she's never met. Knowing he needs her help, she invites him to Havenwood Falls to run a music camp sponsored by her store. As soon as he arrives, she senses a darkness gripping his soul and curling its hooks deeper inside him.

In a race to save his soul, Cecelia grows ever closer to Brett. But she must hold tight to her heart, for within this tortured man lies a secret darker than her past, and deadlier than she ever imagined.

ROCK ME GENTLY

AN EXCERPT

"*H*ey, Brett, you ready?"

Brett Rhys-Falwyck, lead guitarist and singer for the band Pink Melon, looked left, then nodded. Looking to his right, he nodded again. Slipping the ear buds into his ears so he could keep in touch with their sound crew, he stepped forward and pulled the microphone closer. Striking the opening chord of their multi-platinum hit song "Love Is Like a Memory," he lowered his tone and sang to the enthusiastic screams and cheers from the thousands of fans in the arena as they recognized and approved his song choice.

Lights flashed around them, psychedelic and random, adding a heartbeat to the drumbeat and chords ramping up the audience's enthusiasm. Not that they needed much more to get them dancing. From the minute Brett and the boys of Pink Melon stepped onto the stage and began the opening to their hit that was flooding the airwaves, the audience belonged to them.

Brett's body gyrated provocatively, caught up in the deep bass and fast rhythms of the song and sending the audience into a frenzy of movement that matched his subtle sexuality. He didn't notice. Throwing his head back and hips forward, he strummed his guitar with a fierce desire to wring every note from the instrument, as if stroking a lover's body. Smooth and sure, his fingers slid and caressed each string, pulling from the guitar the emotion of the song as if he were playing for every woman in the audience individually.

He ignored the whistles and screams from the bobbing crowd below the stage, focusing instead on the song's words and their meaning, trying to draw every bit of feeling out of the song that he could. Nothing stopped him when he became like this. He smiled as the spotlights flashed on and off the other band members, keeping them in both shadow and light, further adding to the unreality of being in a full house with adoring fans screaming their names. He saw his bandmates, all of them friends for quite a while before the band hit it big, enjoying the music and adulation from the crowd as much as he was. Were they inspired by his energy, or by their own connection to the music? In the end, that wasn't as important as giving the audience what they paid for.

The audience was hearing even more than that tonight. His body absorbed the music, the tune singing in his blood and lending a fire to his playing he hadn't heard before. He was inspired to be greater, his late mother's presence all around him, comforting and familiar, pushing him to new heights. He felt nine years old again with his first guitar playing just to her, even though the audience in front of him strained for his attention.

This particular song was one he and the band had argued about before coming on stage. He wanted to open with it, but the others wanted to end with it, to keep the audience anticipating whether they would play it or not. He'd won that particular battle as scheduling the set order was his thing, after all. He instinctively knew what the crowd would go for, and he'd yet to be proven wrong.

The song was up for a Grammy Award and very popular at concerts even though, as a ballad, it was very different from most of what they played. Pink Melon wasn't known for playing love songs. Their fans expected more rock and roll with hard chords and riffs, but this song had somehow captured the attention of radio stations across the country, and that had led to fans requesting it on the online outlets. Their music video had over a million views, all of which helped shoot the song up the charts and skyrocket the band to prominence.

Their newest album would have more ballads and less rock and roll due to his songs. That had led to a bit of discord among the guys.

Grumbling, they'd played their parts, sang his lyrics, but still they didn't like the direction the band was going. Brett was sure they would be talking about this for a while before they went on tour again, this time to bigger houses, they hoped. No more college campuses or state fairs or small venues unless they chose them.

Brett leaned into the microphone, his mouth nearly sucking it like a lollipop as he locked eyes with a pretty redhead in the crowd. She danced for him as he sang, her large boobs nearly falling out of her low-cut T-shirt as she sought to keep his attention. The light moved on, and she was lost to view in the sudden darkness.

The crowd cheered and sang along to the popular tune. The song, one Brett had penned when in one of his rare romantic moments, had become such a sensation that the band was nonstop busy these days. No one was complaining. Playing to sold-out houses had been the goal of Pink Melon from the beginning, after all. Rock and roll might be what put them together, but romantic ballads like this one were going to pay the bills. They all knew it—didn't like it, but knew it.

As the song progressed, Brett alternately singing and strumming his guitar to the subtle rhythms of the unique love song, the rest of the band played to the crowd with their own enthusiastic gyrations and musical accompaniments.

The crowd cheered enthusiastically every time Cooly dipped his guitar or flipped his long blond hair like an eighties rocker. The other band members—drummer Peter "Sticks" Friend and their keyboardist Harry Williams—also bobbed and swayed to the music.

Brett glanced out into the nearly invisible audience. The redhead, if she was still there, was hidden in the glare of the lights. He couldn't see anyone in particular right now, just indefinable shapes as the lights scanned the crowd like a police helicopter, making individual faces impossible to differentiate. Closing his eyes to lose the feeling of vertigo that always struck him when on stage, he took a deep breath and focused on his guitar and the music instead of the overexcited fans.

The combination of the footlights, hot smells from the electrical equipment, the sharp familiar feel of his guitar, and its steel strings on his fingers lulled him into a kind of melodic trance. He knew where he was, but he became lost in his music—a trait reporters following the music scene called his "harmonic haze," but which he called his "escape." Music had always been a way to express thoughts and emotions too painful or uncomfortable to talk about face to face with the people in his life.

Shy and a bit of a loner, starting a band was a way to challenge himself out of his shell. His mother had often despaired of ever receiving grandchildren from her shy only child, and her recent death from cancer made that a real regret for him. Biting his lip, he relished the pain that kept him in the moment. Fighting back the tears that threatened to fall at the thought of his mother, he closed his eyes, taking deep ragged breaths to regain control of his emotions. How she would have loved to be here, front and center, for his performance. He regretted so much in life, nothing more than the fact that she would never be here to share this with him.

His focus returned to the strings, the solidness of the guitar, and the energy he felt in the air around him as he put the sadness of his mother's death behind him. His heart pounding, his body vibrating with the release music always brought to him, his attention returned to the music.

Every time he sang this song, he felt he was sending out a message to someone, but who? Someone he'd never met? Someone he wanted to meet? He was never sure, but he knew—judging by the thousands of posts and Twitter comments from lonely women and men too—that his message of love being lost and searched for was reaching into the souls of the people he sang to.

So many lonely people.

And he was one of them.

PURCHASE *ROCK ME Gently* at your favorite book store.

www.ingramcontent.com/pod-product-compliance
Lightning Source LLC
Chambersburg PA
CBHW052003170626
46808CB00007B/2760